LIGHTHOUSE COTTAGES

STARLIGHT SHORES
BOOK ONE

KAY CORRELL

ZURA LU PUBLISHING LLC

Published by Zura Lu Publishing LLC

between series - with Josephine and Paul from The Letter.)

LIGHTHOUSE POINT ~ THE SERIES
Wish Upon a Shell - Book One
Wedding on the Beach - Book Two
Love at the Lighthouse - Book Three
Cottage near the Point - Book Four
Return to the Island - Book Five
Bungalow by the Bay - Book Six
Christmas Comes to Lighthouse Point - Book Seven

CHARMING INN ~ Return to Lighthouse Point
One Simple Wish - Book One
Two of a Kind - Book Two
Three Little Things - Book Three
Four Short Weeks - Book Four
Five Years or So - Book Five
Six Hours Away - Book Six
Charming Christmas - Book Seven

SWEET RIVER ~ THE SERIES
A Dream to Believe in - Book One
A Memory to Cherish - Book Two
A Song to Remember - Book Three
A Time to Forgive - Book Four
A Summer of Secrets - Book Five
A Moment in the Moonlight - Book Six

MOONBEAM BAY ~ THE SERIES

The Parker Women - Book One
The Parker Cafe - Book Two
A Heather Parker Original - Book Three
The Parker Family Secret - Book Four
Grace Parker's Peach Pie - Book Five
The Perks of Being a Parker - Book Six

BLUE HERON COTTAGES ~ THE SERIES

Memories of the Beach - Book One
Walks along the Shore - Book Two
Bookshop near the Coast - Book Three
Restaurant on the Wharf - Book Four
Lilacs by the Sea - Book Five
Flower Shop on Magnolia - Book Six
Christmas by the Bay - Book Seven
Sea Glass from the Past - Book Eight

MAGNOLIA KEY ~ THE SERIES

Saltwater Sunrise - Book One
Encore Echoes - Book Two
Coastal Candlelight - Book Three
Tidal Treasures - Book Four
Bayside Beginnings - Book Five
Seaside Sunshine - Book Six
Boardwalk Breezes - Book Seven

STARLIGHT SHORE ~ THE SERIES

Lighthouse Cottages - Book One

CHRISTMAS SEASHELLS AND SNOWFLAKES
Seaside Christmas Wishes
Sweet River Holiday Homecoming

WIND CHIME BEACH ~ A stand-alone novel

INDIGO BAY ~
Sweet Days by the Bay - Kay's Complete Collection of stories in the Indigo Bay series

Sign up for my newsletter at my website *kaycorrell.com* to make sure you don't miss any new releases or sales.

ABOUT THIS BOOK

Her reputation in ruins, her only refuge is a lighthouse with secrets of its own.

After a false accusation of theft shatters her world, art teacher Emily Shaw flees to a quiet cottage on the Gulf Coast. She only wants to hide from the media storm that ruined her life, but the small town of Starlight Harbor has other plans.

Among the Lighthouse Cottage residents, Emily finds unexpected allies in the wise lighthouse keeper, Winnie, and her protective nephew, Cliff. But Grant Stone, the handsome local gallery owner, is wary of outsiders with artistic ambitions, especially one with a past as notorious as Emily's.

When Emily uncovers an old lighthouse journal hinting at hidden family secrets, she's drawn deeper into Starlight Harbor's tight-knit community. As she cautiously begins painting again, her art transforms into something raw and honest she's never created before.

When her past comes roaring back with the threat of a new lawsuit, Emily must choose between running again or finding the courage to exhibit her deeply personal new work and fight for her name. In a place where the tide reveals all, she must learn that redemption comes not from proving her innocence to the world, but from the light she finds within herself.

CHAPTER 1

Emily Shaw had spent the last six months being called a thief and a fraud, but the Lockhart Lighthouse didn't seem to care about her ruined reputation. It rose before her, its white tower catching the first rays of the sunset, and she gripped the steering wheel hard enough to feel the stitching dig into her palms.

After two days of driving, sleeping in rest stop parking lots, and living on gas station coffee, she'd arrived at a lighthouse at the edge of the Gulf, standing watch over water that stretched endlessly toward the horizon.

She'd made it. She'd actually made it to the edge of the world, or at least far enough from Chicago that maybe the whispers couldn't follow.

The rental listing hadn't done the lighthouse justice. Against the amber sky, the lighthouse looked eternal. Emily pulled her beat-up Honda into the parking area. Crushed shells and stones crunched beneath her tires. A pelican lifted off from a nearby post, its wings catching the last light as it glided toward the water.

She cut the engine. Sat there. Watched another pelican follow the first, then a third, their silhouettes dark against the fading sky. Counting gave her something to do besides think.

The engine ticked as it cooled. She should get out. Grab her bag. Walk up to the keeper's quarters and pretend to be the kind of person who belonged in a place like this.

Instead, she pressed her forehead against the steering wheel and counted her breaths.

One step at a time. Just get through tonight.

She grabbed a suitcase that held enough for a night, the bare minimum she'd need, and headed toward the keeper's quarters. Her sneakers caught on an uneven flagstone, and she threw her hand out, catching herself hard against the porch railing. Her palm stung. She stood there for a moment, steadying herself, then climbed the remaining steps.

The front door opened before she could knock.

A woman stood silhouetted in the doorway, silver hair swept into a neat bun. She looked Emily up and down in a single efficient sweep, taking in the wrinkled clothes, the unwashed hair pulled into a messy ponytail, and the dark circles that hadn't faded in months.

"You must be Emily Shaw." The woman's voice carried a hint of coastal drawl softened by years. "I'm Winifred Lockhart, though everyone calls me Winnie. You look like you could use some coffee."

Emily opened her mouth to decline. She didn't want coffee and didn't want conversation, but Winnie had already turned and walked inside, clearly expecting her to follow.

She followed.

The living room stopped her two steps in. Ship wheels mounted on the walls. Weathered maps framed behind glass. Faded photographs of lighthouses covering every available surface. Brass fixtures. A compass in a wooden case. A whole museum's worth of maritime history crammed into one room.

The smell hit her next, with the aroma of strong coffee cutting through something older. Wood polish, salt air, decades of weather seeping through the walls. It smelled like a place that had witnessed things and kept them to itself.

Winnie pointed to a kitchen table scarred by decades of use. Knife marks, water rings, and one long gouge that looked like it might have a story. "Sit. You've had a long drive."

Emily sank into the wooden chair. Her legs ached. Her back ached. Everything ached. Winnie placed a mug before her, and she wrapped her hands around it, letting the heat seep into her fingers.

The coffee was strong enough to strip paint, which was exactly what she needed.

Winnie settled across from her, her own mug cupped in weathered hands. She didn't speak immediately. The silence stretched between them, not uncomfortable, but watchful. Assessing.

"The cottage is ready for you," Winnie finally said. "Starfish Cottage. It's the smallest and oldest, but it has the best light." She paused, and something flickered across her face. "North-facing windows in a small studio space. My father added them years ago for an artist friend who never quite made it down here. Most people use the studio as a sitting room now."

Emily's fingers tightened on the mug. The heat bordered on painful, but she didn't let go.

Studio space. North-facing windows.

She took a long sip of coffee and said nothing.

Winnie watched her over the rim of her own mug. Her sharp eyes didn't miss much. But Winnie didn't press. Didn't ask questions. Just sat there with the patience of someone who had learned that waiting told you more than asking.

"Storage," Emily said finally. "I could use it for storage."

Winnie's expression didn't change. "Of course. Whatever suits you."

They finished their coffee in silence. Outside, the sky shifted from amber to rose to deep purple, and the lighthouse began to glow against the darkening horizon.

Winnie rose, moving with the careful precision of someone who'd learned to accommodate age without surrendering to it. "Come on. I'll show you to your cottage before it gets too dark."

Emily followed her out the side door and into a courtyard that stopped her in her tracks.

Six cottages sat in a gentle semicircle around a garden wild with coastal plants she couldn't name. Spiky things and trailing things and something with small purple flowers that had gone leggy in the salt air. Fairy lights strung between posts cast a warm glow against the gathering dusk. Stone paths connected everything. A fire pit centered the space, surrounded by mismatched chairs. Adirondack, wicker, and one that looked like it might have been rescued from a shipwreck. A gazebo sat at one edge, its archway leading to a path that disappeared toward the sound of waves.

Emily stood there, her suitcase hanging from her hand.

"Each cottage has its own personality." Pride crept into Winnie's voice as they crossed the courtyard.

"Starfish is there on the end. Heron Cottage next to it. That one's empty right now. Then Captain's Watch, Sea Glass, Compass Rose, and Driftwood Cottage."

She pointed to each in turn, her hand steady despite her age. When she indicated the last cottage, her hand lingered slightly longer. Her voice went quieter.

"My nephew Clint lives there. He maintains the property and keeps an eye on things."

Emily filed that away. The pause. The careful word choice. The way Winnie's shoulders pulled back when she mentioned her nephew. There were stories here, she could tell. Stories nobody talked about openly.

She was becoming an expert at recognizing that kind of silence. She lived inside one herself.

"The other residents keep various hours," Winnie continued, resuming her walk. "Melissa in Captain's Watch is a photographer. Tends to prowl around at odd times. Early mornings, late nights. You might see her with her camera when you least expect it."

They reached Starfish Cottage. The paint was a soft blue-gray that had weathered into something between sky and sea. Not shabby, but worn smooth, like a stone tumbled by waves until all its sharp edges were gone.

Winnie produced an old-fashioned key, the kind Emily hadn't seen in years. Heavy iron, oxidized to a greenish patina. It slid into the lock with a solid click.

The door opened to reveal a space that somehow felt immediately like somewhere she could hide and somewhere that might ask too much of her, both at the same time.

The main room combined living and kitchen areas, furnished simply but comfortably. A faded floral sofa faced windows that looked out toward the lighthouse. A kitchen table sat in the corner where morning light would fall across it. Everything looked gently worn. Not run-down but lived-in. The kind of worn that came from decades of people actually using things instead of just looking at them.

Emily set her suitcase down. Her eyes went immediately to the doorway on the right. The one Winnie hadn't mentioned yet.

"Bedroom and bath through there." Winnie pointed to the left. "Studio's to the right, though you can use it for whatever you like." She paused. "Storage, maybe. Like you said."

Storage. She almost laughed out loud. Before everything that had happened, she couldn't imagine giving up a studio space for storage. But now? It sounded like a practical suggestion.

"The lighthouse has been in my family for generations." Winnie moved to the window, gazing out at the structure now beginning to glow against the darkening sky. "It's seen a lot of changes and weathered a lot of storms. Hurricane seasons that stripped the paint right off. But it kept standing. Kept doing what it was built to do."

Winnie turned back to her, those sharp eyes seeming to see straight through to everything Emily wasn't saying. "People tend to sort themselves out here. When they're ready."

Emily's jaw ached. She unclenched it deliberately. "I'm just here to rest."

"Of course." Winnie moved toward the door. "There's a community get-together on Fridays if you're inclined. Fire pit in the courtyard. Nothing fancy. Not required. Nothing's required here except respect for the property and each other."

She paused at the threshold, her hand resting on the frame.

"Oh, and Emily? The lighthouse beam still operates. Automated now, of course. No one needs to climb those stairs anymore. But it'll sweep past your windows every forty-five seconds once full dark falls." She glanced back. "Some find it comforting. Others need blackout curtains. There's a set in the bedroom closet if you need them."

Then she was gone. The door closed softly behind her.

Emily stood alone in the cottage. She counted her breaths. In for four, hold for four, out for four. The therapist she'd seen exactly three times had taught her that. Before she'd stopped going. Before she'd stopped being able to afford it.

She tossed her jacket toward a chair. Missed. It slid to the floor, and she left it there.

The window drew her. She crossed to it and looked out at the lighthouse, its white tower now glowing faintly against a sky that had deepened to purple. Somewhere, a bird called out, sharp and mournful.

She should unpack. Get settled. Make the cottage feel less like a hiding place and more like something else. The word home felt foreign. She hadn't had a home in months. She'd had places she slept, places she stored her things, places she existed. But home? She wasn't sure she knew what that meant anymore.

Her suitcase sat on the bed in the bedroom. The zipper fought her until she finally yanked it open hard enough to break one of the teeth.

She stared at the contents. Clothes grabbed without thinking, whatever had been closest. A sweater she hated. Three shirts she hadn't worn in years. One pair of pants that actually fit. She hung a few items in the closet and dumped the rest in the dresser. Good enough.

Toiletries in the bathroom. The medicine cabinet mirror showed her a face she barely recognized. Pale, drawn, older than it had the right to look. She shut the cabinet door without studying herself further.

Then she was back in the main room, facing the studio door.

Just a door. Nothing special about a door. Pine, with a small nick in the frame where something had bumped against it once. A crystal doorknob that caught what little light remained.

Her hand reached for the knob before she could think better of it.

The studio took her breath away.

North-facing windows dominated the far wall, their glass so clean it seemed to disappear. The last traces of twilight filtered through, painting everything in that perfect golden light that artists called the magic hour. Built-in shelves lined one wall, waiting for supplies she didn't have. An easel stood in the corner like an accusation.

She stepped inside. The floorboards creaked under her weight.

It was a proper studio. The kind of space she'd dreamed about during art school, when she'd shared a cramped corner of a converted warehouse with three other students and called herself lucky. The kind of space she'd worked toward for fifteen years. The kind of space she'd finally achieved, briefly, before everything fell apart.

How long had it been since she'd actually painted?

Eight months? More? She'd tried, once, in the cramped corner of the Chicago apartment after she'd been let go. She'd squeezed ultramarine onto her palette, picked up a brush, and then nothing. Her hand had refused to move. Three hours she'd sat there, the paint drying on the palette, the canvas blank in front of her. Then she'd cleaned her brushes, packed them away, and hadn't touched them since.

"Fraud," she whispered into the empty studio.

She blinked. The windows that had seemed so beautiful now felt like eyes watching her, waiting for her to pretend she belonged here.

Her hand found the doorknob. She stepped backward into the main room, pulling the door closed behind her. Her fingers found the lock and pushed it into place.

There. Problem solved.

She stood with her palm flat against the closed door, feeling the grain of the wood under her fingers.

The bedroom felt safer. Anonymous. She could be anyone in here. Just another rental tenant running from something, no different from dozens of others who'd probably slept in this bed and stared at this same ceiling.

The mattress dipped under her weight as she sat. The quilt was soft, faded. A wedding ring pattern in blues and greens that reminded her of the Gulf water she'd driven past this morning. She ran her fingers along the stitching. Someone had made this by hand once. Someone had chosen these fabrics, cut these shapes, and sewn them together with care.

Through the window, she caught her first glimpse of the lighthouse beam.

It swept across the water, slow and steady. A bright arc cutting through the darkness, then gone. She counted. Forty-five seconds later, it came again. And again.

She kicked off her shoes. One landed by the closet door. The other bounced off the dresser and disappeared underneath it. She considered retrieving it. Didn't.

Instead, she lay back on the bed, still fully dressed. The quilt bunched under her shoulder, and she shifted until it smoothed out. Above her, the ceiling was plain white plaster.

The lighthouse beam swept past again, throwing a brief stripe of light across the ceiling. She tracked its movement with her eyes. It appeared at the left edge of the window and slid across, disappearing to the right.

Forty-five seconds.

Everything else in her life had proven unreliable, like her mentor's legacy, her husband's loyalty, and her own reputation. But this light circled back exactly when promised.

But this light. This light came back exactly when promised.

The beam swept past. She counted. Forty-five seconds. Again. Forty-five seconds.

Her eyes grew heavy. She should get up. Brush her teeth. Change into pajamas like a functional adult. Instead, she pulled the edge of the quilt over herself, not quite ready to commit to being here but too exhausted to be anywhere else.

The lighthouse beam swept past.

Forty-five seconds.

Forty-five seconds.

Somewhere between counts, sleep claimed her. Her last thought was that Winnie had been right about one thing.

Some people would find the lighthouse beam comforting.

Emily just hadn't expected to be one of them.

CHAPTER 2

Emily woke to sunlight streaming through her cottage windows and the sound of waves rolling onto shore. For a moment, she lay still, letting the peacefulness wash over her. Then yesterday's events came flooding back—the long drive, Winnie's knowing eyes, the studio door she'd locked because she couldn't bear to look at it.

She sat up slowly, testing the feeling. No upset stomach. No immediate urge to pack her bags and run. Just a quiet morning in a cottage by a lighthouse, as far from Chicago as she could manage.

Her phone showed a single notification. She braced herself before checking it.

An email from her lawyer. Subject line: "Holloway Update."

She punched the delete button without reading the email. Whatever Julian Holloway was doing now, she didn't want to know. That was the whole point of running away—no, *traveling*—to Florida.

She forced herself out of bed and into the shower, letting the hot water wash away the grogginess of sleeping in her clothes. When she emerged, she felt slightly more human. She pulled on clean shorts and a soft t-shirt, then ventured into the small kitchen to make coffee.

The coffee maker was ancient but functional. While it gurgled and hissed, she stood at the window watching the morning light play across the lighthouse. The white paint seemed to glow in the early sun, and she found herself cataloging details automatically. She noted the way the cylindrical form caught the light, the contrast between the smooth tower and rough stone base, and the delicate ironwork of the gallery railing.

Stop analyzing it like you're going to paint it. You don't paint anymore.

A knock at her door interrupted the familiar spiral of self-recrimination.

"Emily? It's Winnie. I brought breakfast if you're hungry."

She opened the door to find Winnie holding a basket covered with a blue-checked cloth. The older woman looked fresh and energetic despite the early hour, and her silver hair was neatly braided.

"I hope I'm not intruding. I just thought you might like something more substantial than whatever you managed to pack in that car."

"You're not intruding. Come in. I was just making coffee, but I'm pretty sure it's terrible coffee."

"Then it's a good thing I brought some of my own." Winnie swept into the cottage and began unpacking the basket on the small kitchen table. Fresh blueberry muffins, still warm. Butter. Strawberries. And a thermos that smelled infinitely better than whatever was brewing in Emily's pot.

"You don't have to feed me." Her stomach betrayed her with an audible growl.

"I don't have to do anything. I want to." Winnie poured coffee from her thermos into two mugs. "Besides, I have an ulterior motive. I'm curious about you."

Her defenses rose immediately. "Curious how?"

"Relax, dear. I'm not going to interrogate you." Winnie settled into a chair and gestured for Emily to do the same. "I've had enough residents come through these cottages to recognize someone who's running from something. You don't have to tell me what. But I did want to check that you're all right. That you're not in any danger."

The directness caught her off guard. "I'm not in physical danger. Just... legal complications. And reputational ones."

"Ah." Winnie buttered a muffin and took a bite. "The kind where you did nothing wrong but everyone assumes you did?"

Her throat tightened. "Something like that."

"Well, you'll find that Starlight Shores is a good place for starting over. People here don't much care what the internet says about you."

They ate in comfortable silence for a few minutes. The muffins were tender and sweet with bursts of berry flavor. She realized she hadn't eaten a real meal in days.

"Did the lighthouse light bother you last night?"

"Not at all. I actually… enjoyed it."

"I thought you might. The lighthouse is quite something, isn't it?"

"It's beautiful. The architecture is fascinating. It's late 1800s construction, I'd guess?"

"1885. My great-great-grandfather helped build it, and the Lockharts have been keepers ever since. Four generations, including me." Pride colored Winnie's voice.

"That's remarkable. Not many families maintain that kind of continuity."

"It's in our blood, I suppose. The lighthouse, the Gulf, this stretch of coast. My father used to say the lighthouse called to the people who needed it most." Winnie smiled. "Of course, he said a lot of peculiar things. I found some of his old papers while cleaning the storage room last week. They were full of the most cryptic entries about signals. Probably just the musings of someone who spent too much time alone with his thoughts."

Her curiosity stirred despite herself. "What kind of signals?"

"Oh, who knows. Lighthouse keepers had their own language, I suppose. Most of it's lost to time now." Winnie shrugged and began gathering the breakfast things. "Oh, and Emily? You should take a walk this morning. The beach is lovely, and fresh air does wonders for spiraling thoughts."

After Winnie left, Emily stood at the window with her second cup of coffee. The lighthouse beam had stopped its rotation, replaced by ordinary daylight.

Her phone buzzed in her pocket. She almost ignored it, but the persistence of the vibration made her check.

A text from a number she didn't recognize: *Ms. Shaw, this is Julian Holloway's attorney. We need to discuss your continued use of techniques derived from Franklin Holloway's intellectual property. Please contact our office immediately.*

Her hands shook as she read it again. Then again. How did they get her number? She'd changed it before leaving Chicago. Had someone from her old life given it to them?

"You can't run far enough," Julian had threatened during their last confrontation. "I'll make sure everyone knows exactly what you are."

She sat down hard on the couch. She was kidding herself, thinking she could hide here. Julian had found her in Tallahassee within three weeks. He'd tracked her to Mobile in less than two. He'd find her in Starlight Shores eventually.

The only question was whether she'd still be here when he did or if she'd have run again by then.

She pulled up her email app and saw three more messages from addresses she didn't recognize, all with subject lines designed to intimidate her.

Legal Action Pending.

Urgent Response Required.

Final Notice Before Filing.

Harassment. That's all this was. Her lawyer had been clear that Julian had no case. The investigation had cleared her completely. She'd done nothing wrong.

But wrong and guilty were different things in the court of public opinion. And Julian had unlimited resources to keep making her life miserable, even if he couldn't win in actual court.

She thought about Winnie's words. *We tend to judge people by who they are here, not who the internet says they were somewhere else.*

What if she stayed? What if, just once, he didn't find her?

Her phone buzzed again. This time, she deleted the message without reading it. Then blocked the number. Then blocked the email addresses that had been harassing her all morning.

It wouldn't stop Julian. But it would stop her from seeing his threats every five minutes.

CHAPTER 3

The next morning, Winnie knelt in the soft earth of her herb garden, carefully tucking a small rosemary plant into place. Her knees protested the position, but she ignored them. Some aches were worth bearing for the satisfaction of working with her hands. The morning sun warmed her back as she patted the soil around the fragrant herb.

She glanced up at the sound of a door closing. Emily stood on the small porch of Starfish Cottage, hesitating before stepping down into the courtyard. The woman moved like someone expecting the ground to shift beneath her feet, cautious and uncertain. Winnie recognized that look. She'd seen it on countless faces over the decades.

"Good morning. Beautiful day, isn't it?" She kept her voice light and casual. No need to spook the woman. She pushed herself to her feet and brushed the soil from her gardening gloves.

Emily nodded, her gaze darting around the courtyard as if checking for other people. "It is." Emily hesitated, then stepped closer. "The garden. It's beautiful. Did you design this?"

"Over many years. The garden changes with the seasons, just like the people who come here."

"How long have you been the lighthouse keeper?"

She rose and stretched. "Officially? About fifty years now. Unofficially, I've been part of this lighthouse my entire life."

Emily's eyebrows rose. "Fifty years? That's impressive. I didn't realize lighthouses were still family operations."

"Most aren't anymore. The Coast Guard automated many of them years ago. We fought to maintain private ownership when they decommissioned it. The light still works. It's just not the primary navigational aid it once was."

"It must be special, having that kind of family legacy."

"Special and sometimes heavy. Each generation of Lockharts has faced its own challenges in keeping this place alive. The cottages were my solution. We had Starfish Cottage, but I begged my father to add the others over the years."

"Your solution?"

"Lighthouse upkeep isn't cheap. The rent from the cottages helps with expenses. And I'm always getting offers from developers who want to buy the property, change it, and make it into something it wasn't meant to be. The extra income helps keep them at bay."

"Developers want to buy the lighthouse?"

"And the cottages, though I'm sure they'd tear them down and put up some big resort." She shook her head. "But more importantly, I realized the lighthouse had always been a beacon for those needing direction. The cottages just formalized what was already happening naturally."

"What do you mean?" Emily's brow creased.

"People find their way here when they need something." She brushed dirt from her gloves. "Most of them don't know what it is yet."

Emily tensed. "I'm just looking for some peace and quiet."

"Of course. That's how it starts."

"How what starts?"

"Figuring out what you actually want." She motioned toward the other cottages. "Take Melissa in Captain's Watch. Professional photojournalist. Covered disasters worldwide. Now she only photographs the lighthouse at dawn. Or Clint in Driftwood Cottage—came back after twenty years in the Coast Guard because this was the only place that made sense anymore."

Emily shifted uncomfortably. "I'm not planning to stay that long."

"Few do, at first."

Emily glanced back at her cottage, obviously looking for an escape. "I was thinking of heading into town to get a few things."

"Bayview General Store has most essentials. If you want breakfast, Harbor Brew downtown makes the best coffee in three counties. Marty Fuller at Tides & Tales bookstore can recommend local history books if you're interested in the area or if you want to pick up a good fiction read."

"Thank you. I appreciate the information."

She could see the walls the younger woman had built around herself, sturdy as a fortress made of stones. Whatever had happened to Emily Shaw had taught her to guard herself carefully. Winnie recognized the signs because she'd spent decades perfecting her own defenses.

"As I mentioned earlier, we have a small gathering in the courtyard most Friday evenings. Nothing fancy, just wine and conversation. You're welcome to join us whenever you feel like company."

Emily's expression tightened. "I'm not really looking for social activities right now."

"Of course. The invitation stands whenever you're ready. No pressure at all. And privacy is respected here. Whatever brought you to Starfish

Cottage is your business. You'll find no prying questions from me."

Something in Emily's eyes softened slightly at that. Perhaps she'd expected Winnie to push or demand explanations or participation. So many people did, never understanding that healing couldn't be rushed.

"I should head into town now."

Winnie nodded and watched Emily head toward her car. There was a story there, one written in the set of the woman's shoulders and the shadows beneath her eyes. She had developed an instinct over the years for recognizing pain in others, even when they tried to hide it.

She turned back to her gardening, pulling a stubborn weed from beside the rosemary. Emily reminded her of the lighthouse during a storm—still standing but battered by waves. That kind of determination took tremendous strength, but it also exacted a price. She knew that cost all too well.

Emily would find her way in time. The lighthouse had never failed to help lost souls rediscover their bearings. Some people needed space before they could accept connection. She'd learned that lesson through decades of watching people arrive broken and leave whole.

The drive into downtown Starlight Shores took less than five minutes. Emily followed Winnie's directions to the historic district, parking on a tree-lined street near the harbor. The town was exactly as charming as she feared it would be. Colorful buildings lined the waterfront, their facades freshly painted in cheerful blues, yellows, and coral. Flower boxes overflowed with blooms and trailing vines. It looked like a postcard or a movie set and almost too perfect to be real.

She walked slowly along the main street, taking in the shops and restaurants. The bookstore Winnie had recommended, Tides & Tales, occupied a corner building with large windows displaying maritime histories and local authors. Close by, a seafood restaurant called The Sandpiper advertised fresh catch and sunset specials. Everything about the town radiated authenticity and history, the kind of place that had been here for generations and planned to remain for generations more.

Bayview General Store sat in the middle of the block, its wooden sign weathered but freshly painted. Emily took a breath before pushing through the door, triggering a cheerful bell.

The interior was packed with everything from fishing supplies to gourmet food items, organized in a way that suggested decades of evolution rather than any particular plan. An older woman behind the counter looked up with a welcoming smile.

"Good morning. You must be the woman staying at the lighthouse."

She blinked, caught off guard by the immediate recognition. "I am. How did you know?"

"Small town, honey. Word travels fast when Winnie gets a new tenant." The woman's smile widened, and she winked. "And Winnie called to say you might be stopping by and to help you get stocked up. I'm Sally Morris, by the way. My family has run this store for years. If you need anything, you just ask."

Word travels fast. She managed a smile. Wonderful. By tomorrow, they'd probably know her shoe size and her credit score. Maybe they could skip ahead to the part where they ran her out of town and save everyone some time.

"Thank you. I'm Emily." She left off her last name, hoping to maintain at least a shred of anonymity.

"Welcome to Starlight Shores. The lighthouse and its cottages are a special place. You picked a good spot to land."

She nodded, unsure how to respond to that. She grabbed a basket and started gathering supplies, acutely aware of Sally's friendly gaze following her progress through the store. Two other customers, both older women, studied her with undisguised curiosity.

She pretended not to notice and focused intently

on comparing the prices of pasta sauce. She'd known a small town would mean less privacy, but she hadn't expected to become a topic of conversation quite so quickly.

She paid for her purchases, enduring Sally's cheerful chatter about an upcoming festival and how Emily simply must attend. Outside, she loaded her bags into the car and stood for a moment, debating whether to head straight back to the cottage or push through her discomfort and explore a bit more.

Coffee. She needed coffee.

Winnie had mentioned Harbor Brew. The coffee shop was easy to spot a block down, its large windows offering views of the harbor. Emily left her groceries in the car and slowly walked toward it.

Just coffee. She was just getting coffee.

Harbor Brew's interior matched the rest of the town with its nautical decor and exposed brick walls. The scent of fresh-brewed coffee and baked goods made her stomach growl. A handful of customers occupied tables near the windows, and a short line had formed at the counter.

She joined the line and studied the menu board while she tried not to notice the curious glances from other patrons. She was definitely the new person in town, marked as clearly as if she wore a sign.

"Morning, Grant." A woman greeted the man ahead of Emily with easy familiarity. "The usual?"

"Please. And one of those cranberry scones, if you have any left."

Her attention snapped to the man in front of her. He was tall, probably a few inches over six feet, with dark hair touched with silver at the temples. He wore shorts and a blue button-down shirt with the sleeves rolled up, revealing tanned forearms. There was something solid and capable about him, and he stood with easy confidence in a space he clearly knew well.

He turned slightly as he reached for his wallet, and their eyes met.

The impact was immediate and unexpected. His eyes were a deep blue-gray, intelligent and assessing. For a moment, something flickered between them. Recognition? Attraction?

Then his expression shifted, a subtle closing off that she recognized all too well. His gaze sharpened with what looked like wariness, maybe even suspicion. *He knew who she was. Somehow, he knew.*

Or there was always the possibility she was imagining it…

"Here you go, Grant." The woman—Jan, if her name tag wasn't lying—handed him his coffee and scone.

"Thanks, Jan." He nodded politely to Emily, a

gesture of acknowledgment that felt more like dismissal, and headed for the door.

She watched him leave, her heart still racing. Whatever warmth she'd glimpsed in that first moment had vanished, replaced by the cool distance of someone who'd already decided what to think of her.

Well, at least he was efficient about it. He'd managed it in under five seconds. That had to be some kind of record.

"What can I get you?" Jan's friendly voice pulled Emily back to the present.

"Large coffee, black, please. And… one of those cranberry scones?"

"You're in luck. I've got one cranberry scone left." Jan reached for a bag. "You visiting for a bit?"

"Yes, staying at the Lighthouse Cottages." She managed a smile, wondering if everyone in Starlight Shores was going to ask her about her business.

"Winnie's place is wonderful. Such a special property." Jan smiled as she got the order ready.

She paid and took her coffee and scone, grateful for something to hold. She should leave, go back to the cottage where she could be alone. She stepped outside, where she could see the man from the coffee shop walking down the street. Grant. Jan had called him Grant.

He moved with purpose, carrying his coffee and the bag with his scone, and heading toward a building near the end of the block. She stepped outside and followed at a distance, telling herself she was just exploring the town, not trailing a stranger who'd looked at her with such immediate wariness.

Stone's Gallery. The sign was elegant but understated, much like the building itself. A renovated warehouse with large windows and exposed brick. Through the glass, Emily could see white walls displaying paintings and sculptures, carefully curated and beautifully lit.

She stopped across the street, sipping her coffee and studying the gallery.

He moved inside the gallery with the confidence of ownership, setting down his coffee before approaching a large canvas leaning against the wall. She watched as he carefully lifted it, studying the painting from different angles before positioning it on the wall. His movements were precise and deliberate, the actions of someone who understood exactly how to showcase art to its best advantage. This was his gallery, then?

Despite herself, she felt drawn to the scene. There was something in the way he handled the artwork with reverence and care that spoke to a deep appreciation for the creative process. He adjusted the painting minutely, stepped back to assess it, then made another small correction.

She missed this. The ache of it surprised her. The world of galleries and exhibitions, the careful curation of work, and the anticipation of sharing art with people who understood it. She'd lost all of that along with her reputation.

Grant turned suddenly toward the window, as if sensing her watching him. She spun away quickly and walked in the opposite direction.

Silly. She was being silly, standing there staring into a stranger's gallery like some kind of stalker. What did she expect to find? Answers? Acceptance? Neither of those things waited for her in Starlight Shores or anywhere else.

She made it back to her car, slipped inside, and sat for a moment with her hands on the steering wheel. The morning's expedition had been more draining than a simple supply run should have been. The curious looks, the whispered comments, and the way Grant had looked at her with that flash of recognition, followed by immediate withdrawal, were all too familiar, too reminiscent of the past months when she'd become an outcast in her own professional community.

As if mocking her, her phone dinged with a text message from an unknown number: *Urgent. Open immediately.*

She blocked the number, started the car, and drove back toward the lighthouse, fighting the urge to just keep driving until she hit a state line, then another one. But she had nowhere else to go. Her savings were limited, and her options even more so.

The cottage represented the closest thing she had to a refuge.

The lighthouse came into view as she rounded the last curve, its white tower stark against the blue sky. Something about its solid presence steadied her. It had stood there for over a century. That counted for something.

Maybe that was enough for now. A place to stay, a roof over her head, and the promise that no one would demand more from her than she could give. Winnie had said privacy was respected at the lighthouse. She desperately hoped that was true.

She parked in the parking lot and carried her groceries inside, grateful not to encounter anyone in the courtyard. The cottage welcomed her with its quiet simplicity. She put away her supplies, placed her scone on a small plate, and settled onto the small sofa.

Through the window, she could see the edge of the courtyard, and beyond it, the lighthouse tower. The lighthouse that attracted artists and other lost souls, according to Winnie. She wasn't sure she qualified as either anymore. She'd been an artist once, before everything fell apart. Now she was just someone trying to survive each day without falling completely apart. Okay, maybe the lost soul part fit her.

Her phone buzzed with a text from her lawyer.

She ignored it. Whatever news he had could wait. Everything could wait.

She closed her eyes and listened to the distant sound of waves. In Chicago, she'd lived with the constant noise of traffic, sirens, and the elevated train rattling past her apartment. Here, the silence was broken only by the sounds of the wind, waves, and seabirds calling.

She'd have to get used to it. This was her life now, at least for the foreseeable future. A small cottage, a small town, and the growing certainty that she couldn't hide from her past, no matter how far she ran.

The image of Grant's face flashed through her mind. That moment of connection was followed by immediate retreat. She wondered what he'd heard about her, what version of her story had reached this small Gulf Coast town. Probably the worst version, the one that painted her as a fraud and a thief.

She opened her eyes and stared at the locked studio door. It could wait.

CHAPTER 4

A few days later, Emily stood at the edge of the farmer's market, clutching her canvas bag and wondering if this had been a mistake. The morning sun cut between the vendor stalls, and the scent of fresh bread mingled with the salt air. She'd waited until late morning, hoping the early crowds would have thinned, but the market still buzzed with activity.

"Just get what you need and leave." She adjusted her sunglasses and stepped into the flow of shoppers.

The first stall offered local honey, and she paused to examine the golden jars. The vendor, an older woman with weathered hands, smiled warmly.

"New to town?" The woman tilted her head toward the lighthouse barely visible in the distance. "I saw you walking up from that direction."

"Just visiting." She selected a small jar and handed over exact change, hoping to discourage further conversation.

She moved quickly through the market, gathering fresh herbs and a loaf of sourdough. Each transaction felt like exposure, and every friendly question a potential threat to her anonymity. Maybe she should have driven to the next town for groceries instead, but she could never pass up a farmer's market with its fresh produce and interesting craft displays.

At the pottery stall, she lingered despite herself. A mug caught her eye, glazed in swirling blues and greens that captured the Gulf's shifting colors. She picked it up, running her thumb along the smooth rim.

"Beautiful work." The voice behind her sent a jolt of recognition through her body.

She turned to find Grant standing close enough that she caught the scent of coffee and a hint of his woodsy aftershave. His dark hair caught the morning light, and those blue-gray eyes studied her closely.

"Yes, it is." She set the mug down carefully, fighting the urge to flee.

"Jim does excellent pottery. That glaze technique takes years to master. I feature his work at the gallery sometimes."

She nodded, searching for a polite escape route.

He reached out a hand. "Grant Stone."

Ah, he was the owner of the gallery, like she'd guessed. She reluctantly shook his hand. "Emily." Emily with no last name.

But he wasn't moving away. If anything, he seemed to be examining her face with the same careful attention he might give a painting.

"I thought I recognized you the other day at Harbor Brew." His voice carried a note of discovery that made her watch him carefully. "Couldn't quite place you then, but now…"

She watched the recognition dawn in his eyes, saw the exact moment when he connected her face to whatever he'd seen in those art magazines. His expression shifted, wariness replacing curiosity.

"You're Emily Shaw." Not a question. A statement weighted with everything those words now meant in the art world.

Heat flooded her cheeks. She lifted her chin, meeting his gaze directly even as her hands trembled around the bag handles. "Yes."

She waited for the accusations, the questions about Franklin and the scandal that had destroyed everything she'd built. Instead, Grant's eyes narrowed slightly, as if he were reassessing a painting he'd initially misjudged.

"I read about the situation." His tone remained neutral, but she heard the suspicion underneath. "Must have been difficult."

Difficult. Such a small word for having her life torn apart, her reputation shredded, and her marriage dissolved. She forced a brittle smile. "I should go." She turned to leave, but his voice stopped her.

"Are you planning to stay in Starlight Shores long?"

The question sounded casual, but she heard the real concern beneath it. Was she here to exploit their small town? To use their picturesque lighthouse as a backdrop for some redemptive artistic comeback? She'd seen that look before, in gallery owners who'd once welcomed her and then turned away when the scandal broke.

She met his scrutiny with her own. "I haven't decided. Is that a problem?"

Something flickered in his expression. It wasn't quite hostility, but it certainly wasn't welcome either. "Just curious. We don't get many… established artists here."

The pause before the word "established" felt deliberate, and her defenses snapped into place. "Former artist, you mean. I don't paint anymore."

"No?" His gaze dropped to her hands, and she realized she'd been unconsciously rubbing her thumb against her fingers, the way she used to test paint consistency. "That's a shame. Whatever else happened, you had talent."

Had. Past tense. The word stung more than it

should have from a stranger. "I need to go." She stepped backward, nearly bumping into another shopper. "Excuse me."

She turned and walked away, feeling his eyes on her back. Her hands shook as she gripped the market bag tighter. So much for anonymity. By tomorrow, everyone would know exactly who was staying at Winnie's lighthouse cottage. The disgraced artist. The fraud. The woman who'd betrayed her dying mentor's trust, no matter what the lawyers said.

She quickened her pace, weaving between market stalls toward the parking area. She'd been foolish to think she could disappear in a small town. Grant owned a gallery. He'd have connections throughout the art world and would know all the sordid details of her fall from grace. The way he'd looked at her, measuring and finding her wanting...

"Wait."

Footsteps behind her. She didn't turn, didn't slow down until a hand touched her elbow. The contact sent an unwanted spark through her arm.

"Please." Grant stood beside her now, slightly breathless. "I'm sorry. That came out wrong."

She pulled her arm free, anger replacing embarrassment. "Which part? The part where you implied I'm here to exploit your town? Or where you relegated my entire career to past tense?"

He had the grace to look uncomfortable. Up

close, she could see flecks of cerulean in his eyes, the kind of color that came in tubes labeled sky blue but never quite captured the real thing.

"You're right. I was rude. I get protective. It comes out wrong sometimes."

The admission surprised her. She found herself really looking at him for the first time. She shrugged. "I'm not here to cause trouble. I just needed somewhere to... be."

He nodded slowly. "I understand that. More than you might think."

They stood awkwardly in the parking area while market life swirled around them. She noticed the way he held himself, careful and contained, like someone who'd learned to take up less space than his tall frame required.

"The mug." He nodded toward the pottery stall. "You should go back and get it. Jim's work... it has a way of making morning coffee taste better. He swears it's all about the way he shapes the rim."

It was an olive branch, offered quietly. She hesitated, then nodded. "Maybe I will."

"I'll let you get back to your shopping." He stepped aside, but not before she caught a kind of cautious interest in his expression. "Welcome to Starlight Shores, Emily."

He walked away before she could respond, leaving her standing in the morning sun with a confused mix of attraction and apprehension twisting through her. She watched him navigate the market with easy familiarity, stopping to talk with vendors, his earlier stiffness replaced by genuine warmth.

She returned to the pottery stall and bought the mug. As Jim wrapped it carefully in paper, she tried not to think about the fact that Grant had caught up with her to apologize or the way he'd said her name. Not with accusation, but with a careful neutrality that somehow felt worse.

Back at her cottage, she unpacked her market purchases. The mug she unwrapped slowly, running her fingers over the glazed surface that really did capture something essential about the Gulf waters.

She made tea in her new mug and carried it to the small porch, settling into one of the weathered chairs. The lighthouse stood proud in the afternoon light, its white surface almost blinding in the sun. From here, she could pretend the morning's encounter hadn't happened and that Grant Stone hadn't recognized her and connected her to everything she'd tried to leave behind in Chicago.

But she could still feel his gaze, the careful assessment of someone who knew the art world's harsh realities. He'd create distance now and warn others, perhaps. The small anonymity she'd found would evaporate like morning mist.

"You should leave." She spoke the words aloud,

testing them. "Pack up tonight and find somewhere else."

But where? Another small town where someone else might recognize her? A city where she could disappear but would have to face galleries and artists. Face all the reminders of what she'd lost?

She sipped her tea. It did taste better in the mug. Grant had been right about that, at least. And his look had said he understood exactly what she'd lost and seen through any pretense that she was fine without her art.

Restless, she walked back inside the cottage, still debating whether she should just pack up and leave. The studio door seemed to mock her from inside the cottage.

Still locked. Still untouched.

Maybe Grant's judgment was accurate. Maybe she really was a former artist now, someone who had talent—*past tense*—but lost it along with everything else.

A knock interrupted her spiraling thoughts. She set down the mug and went to the door, expecting Winnie with another gentle invitation to join the community she wasn't ready for.

Instead, she found a small wrapped package on her doorstep. No note, but she recognized the pottery stall's distinctive paper. Inside was a small bowl, glazed in the same layered blues and greens as her mug. Perfect for holding the smooth stones and shells she'd been collecting on her beach walks.

She looked across the courtyard but saw no one. The gift could have been from Jim the potter, a marketing gesture for a new customer. But something told her it wasn't.

She carried the bowl inside and set it on the windowsill, already imagining how the afternoon light would play across its glazed surface. Whatever Grant Stone thought of her past, this small gesture suggested he wasn't ready to condemn her entirely.

But that almost made it worse. Clean rejection, she could handle. This careful kindness from someone immersed in the art world threatened defenses she couldn't afford to lower.

The beautiful bowl was a reminder that she couldn't remain invisible in Starlight Shores. Tomorrow, word would spread. The scandal would follow her here.

She thought again about packing and running. Instead, she filled the bowl with her collected stones and shells and set it where she could see it from her chair.

Grant's boots crunched against the gravel path as he left the lighthouse property behind. He shoved his hands into his pockets, suddenly aware of how empty they felt without the pottery bowl he'd carried all the way from town.

What had he been thinking? A peace offering? An apology?

The afternoon sun slanted through the palm fronds, tossing shifting patterns across the worn path. He'd walked this route a thousand times, knew every dip and curve, every root breaking the earth.

Comfortable. Predictable. Safe.

Unlike whatever impulse had made him purchase that bowl and leave it on Emily Shaw's doorstep.

He told himself it was simple hospitality. The town's reputation depended on welcoming visitors appropriately, even the complicated ones. Especially the complicated ones, actually. Word got around when tourists felt unwelcome, and Starlight Shores needed their business, whether he liked admitting that or not.

But he knew it was more than economic strategy.

Something about her raw defensiveness at the market had gotten under his skin. The way she'd flinched when he'd mentioned her talent in the past tense. That comment had been unkind, even if he'd told himself it was protective. He'd seen genuine hurt flash across her face before she'd masked it with that brittle politeness she seemed to have perfected so well.

He recognized that hurt. Had worn it himself often enough.

He paused where the path met the main road, squinting against the lowering sun. A pickup truck rumbled past, the driver raising two fingers off the steering wheel in the local greeting. Grant returned the gesture automatically.

He started walking again, his pace slower now. The quiet afternoon stretched ahead with no appointments and no obligations. Just the familiar four walls and the artwork of people he trusted. People who'd never left Starlight Shores chasing something bigger and never forgotten where they came from.

People who weren't Emily Shaw, with her expensive education and ruined reputation and eyes that looked like she'd lost something essential. He shouldn't care about any of that.

But Emily's presence unsettled him precisely because she represented everything he'd run from. The art world's politics. The way reputations could be destroyed overnight. The cost of ambition when it collided with integrity, or just bad luck, or someone else's agenda.

But there was something else. A recognition he didn't want to acknowledge.

The way she'd looked at his gallery through the window had struck something deep inside. That hunger mixed with hesitation. That longing for a world she could no longer access. He'd worn that same expression countless times during his first months back in Starlight Shores, standing outside his half-finished gallery space and wondering if he was building something meaningful or just constructing an elaborate hiding place from what had happened with Miranda…

But he didn't think about that anymore. Or at least tried not to. Tried not to remember the betrayal or the way his entire carefully constructed life had collapsed in the span of a single conversation. Tried not to wonder if he'd been running away or running toward something when he'd come home.

He stopped at the gallery's front door, his hand resting on the familiar brass handle. Through the window, he could see the afternoon light pooling across the polished concrete floors and illuminating the carefully curated work of artists he'd handpicked. People he trusted. People who belonged.

He'd built something meaningful here. A space that honored his father's memory while protecting local artists from the kind of exploitation he'd witnessed in New York. A gallery with integrity.

He pulled open the gallery door and stepped

into the familiar quiet. Supporting other artists was his contribution now, and he'd found purpose in showcasing their work instead of creating his own.

Yes, running the gallery was enough.

The lie taunted him.

CHAPTER 5

A restlessness swept through Emily late that afternoon. Grant's recognition of her, the careful way he'd circled around direct questions, and the unexpected gift of the pottery bowl unsettled her.

She stood in the cottage's main room as the afternoon light slanted through the windows. The locked studio door seemed to mock her from across the space. The brief glimpse when she'd first arrived had been enough to send her retreating.

But now, with nervous energy humming through her and nowhere else to direct it, she found herself walking toward that door. Her hand hesitated on the knob. What was she so afraid of? That the space would judge her? That she'd feel her loss of everything that made her who she was, pressing down until she couldn't breathe?

Or maybe she was afraid she'd feel nothing at all.

She unlocked the door, turned the knob, and pushed the door open. The studio greeted her with that perfect north-facing light she'd noticed before. The easel stood like a patient friend. The work table stretched beneath the window, its surface pristine and waiting.

She forced herself to step inside. To breathe. To look around without the panic that had gripped her during her first peek at this space.

The studio was smaller than her space in Chicago had been, but it felt more intimate rather than cramped. Someone had clearly designed it with care. She ran her hand along the work table's edge, noting the quality of the wood and the thoughtful height that would prevent back strain during long sessions.

Built-in cabinets lined one wall, their simple design blending seamlessly with the cottage's coastal aesthetic. She opened them one by one, finding them empty except for a few basic supplies. She discovered brushes, mostly dried out, a palette with ancient paint crusted on its surface, and a small box of charcoal sticks that looked like they'd been there for years.

As she examined the cabinets more closely, something struck her as odd. The proportions seemed inconsistent. Some shelves were deep enough for storing canvases or large supplies, but others were surprisingly narrow. They looked too narrow to be truly useful for art materials. She ran her fingers along one of the shallow shelves, frowning. Why would someone build storage that wasn't practical?

As she knelt to examine the lower cabinets, she noticed small holes drilled through the back wall of one unit. Perfectly round, about the size of her pinky finger, arranged in a pattern that seemed too deliberate to be random. The holes formed what looked like a grid, with some positions filled and others empty. She peered through one of the holes but could only see darkness beyond.

These modifications didn't match the cottage's recent renovations. The wood of these cabinets was older, and the construction style was different from the rest of the space. Someone had built these features long ago, and they'd been preserved through subsequent updates.

But why?

Her gaze drifted to the largest cabinet, the one in the corner that looked heaviest. On impulse, she tried to shift it away from the wall. It barely budged. She braced her feet and pushed harder, feeling it scrape across the floor inch by inch. The effort left her breathing hard, but she'd created enough space to peer behind it.

The wall behind the cabinet looked different

from the rest of the studio. The boards were older and weathered in a way that suggested they'd been exposed to salt air for longer than the cottage itself had existed. She ran her fingers along the seam where two boards met and felt one shift slightly under her touch.

She worked her fingernails into the gap and pulled gently. The board came loose with surprising ease, as if it had been designed to be removable. Behind it, a small compartment had been hollowed out of the wall space between the studs.

Inside, something was wrapped in oilcloth that had yellowed with age. The oilcloth crinkled as she carefully unwrapped it, revealing a book that had been protected from moisture and time. The leather cover was worn but intact, and the pages inside were slightly yellowed but still readable.

She carried it to the work table where the fading light was strongest and opened to the first page. The handwriting was old-fashioned, each letter carefully formed. At the top of the page, an entry that began: "The lighthouse keeper's log should only contain official observations, but these pages will hold the truth of what we do here."

She turned the page, then another, scanning entries that spanned years. Different handwriting appeared throughout, suggesting multiple lighthouse keepers had contributed to this hidden record. Many dates were partially obscured by water damage or faded ink, making it difficult to establish a clear timeline. Some entries were mundane, but others made her pulse quicken.

"Recorded three sequences tonight. Confirmation received."

"Pattern altered as instructed. New protocol in effect."

"Observed unusual activity. Maintained regular intervals despite interference."

"Visitors came by boat. They asked questions about the lighthouse's history. I told them nothing."

Some entries included sketches, rough but clear enough to show architectural details. Modifications to the lighthouse structure. Hidden compartments. What looked like grid patterns with numbers alongside them. Nothing explicitly stated their purpose.

She found herself completely absorbed, turning pages with increasing excitement. This wasn't just a journal. It was a record of something methodical and deliberate, something the lighthouse keepers had been involved in across decades. Her background in art history had included training in archival research, and she recognized the significance of what she'd found. This was a primary source document, carefully preserved and intentionally hidden.

The entries continued with gaps, suggesting either periods of inactivity or missing pages. Then the handwriting changed again, and the entries became more cryptic. References to "sequences" and "patterns" made it difficult to establish a clear timeline.

Winnie's voice called out, interrupting Emily's reading, "Emily? Are you here?"

Her head snapped up. She instinctively moved to cover the journal, then felt foolish. This was Winnie's property. If anyone had a right to know about the journal, it was the lighthouse keeper herself.

"Come in. In the studio."

Winnie appeared in the doorway to the studio, and her gaze swept the room, taking in the moved cabinet and the open journal on the work table. For just a moment, something flickered across Winnie's face. Surprise, maybe. Or fear. Or something Emily couldn't quite name. Then it was gone, replaced by Winnie's usual calm expression.

"I brought you a slice of peach pie," Winnie said, holding up a covered dish. Her eyes drifted to the journal, and this time Emily definitely caught the flash of recognition.

"I found something while I was exploring the studio. There was a hidden compartment behind that cabinet." She watched Winnie's reaction.

"Was there?" Winnie set the dish on a small table near the door and moved closer, her steps measured. "And what did you find in this compartment?"

She motioned to the journal. "This. It looks like a record kept by lighthouse keepers, going back to the early 1900s, maybe earlier. But it's not an official log. It's something else. Something they were hiding."

Winnie reached the work table and looked down at the open pages. Her hand lifted as if to touch the journal, then dropped back to her side. "I see."

The silence stretched between them. She waited, giving Winnie space to explain and claim the journal or perhaps dismiss it as unimportant. But Winnie did neither. She simply stood there, gazing at the pages with an expression Emily couldn't decipher.

"The Lockharts have been the keepers here ever since the lighthouse was built."

"So this journal. It would have been written by your family."

"By my grandfather, yes. And his father before him. And later, my own father." Winnie's finger traced one of the entries. "The lighthouse has served many purposes over the years. Not everything made it into the official logs."

"What kind of purposes?"

"That's a complicated question."

"But you knew this journal existed. That it was hidden here."

"I knew there were more records. I didn't know exactly where they'd all been hidden. My father was protective of the family's secrets. He didn't share everything, even with me. I've spent years trying to piece together the full story. He died suddenly without a chance to explain it all to me."

"What were they doing?"

Winnie pulled out the other chair at the work table and sat down with a small sigh. "I'm not sure. I just know the Lockhart family has always understood their responsibilities. The lighthouse wasn't just a beacon for ships. Sometimes it was a beacon for other purposes. Other needs."

Emily sat back, her mind processing Winnie's words. The journal in front of her wasn't just a historical curiosity. It was evidence of a family legacy that spanned generations.

"The journal is part of a larger story. One I've been trying to piece together for years. I don't know all of it. My father was secretive and protective. He didn't think it was safe to share everything, even with family. Some secrets are kept for good reasons."

"What reasons?"

"To protect people. To keep promises made long ago." Winnie stood slowly. "You have an eye for detail, Emily. An artist's eye. And a researcher's mind. Those entries, the sketches, the coded references are pieces of a puzzle I haven't been able to solve alone. I could use your help figuring it out."

"You want my help?" Surprise washed over her.

"I'm saying that if you choose to look deeper, I won't stop you. But I'm also warning you that some of what you might find could be troubling. There are people who would prefer certain stories stay buried. Who would rather the lighthouse's history remain simple and sanitized."

"The developer?" Emily remembered Winnie's mention of pressure to sell the property.

"Among others." Winnie moved toward the door, then paused. "The journal is yours to study, if you wish. But Emily? Be careful who you share this with. Trust isn't something to give lightly."

She disappeared into the gathering darkness, leaving Emily alone with the journal and a hundred new questions.

She looked down at the pages and the careful handwriting of lighthouse keepers long dead. She ran her gaze across the pages with sketches, codes, and cryptic references that hinted at secrets spanning nearly a century. Her fingers itched to keep reading, to start making notes, to apply her analytical skills to unraveling this mystery.

She turned back to the first page and began reading again.

CHAPTER 6

The morning sun felt warm against Emily's face as she sat on her cottage porch, cradling the pottery mug she'd gotten at the farmers' market. The coffee inside had gone lukewarm while she'd been lost in thought, replaying her discovery of the journal and Winnie's cryptic warnings about people who wanted the lighthouse's secrets to stay buried.

She took a sip anyway and grimaced. Cold coffee was still coffee, though, and she needed the caffeine after staying up half the night reading through the journal's entries. The entries, at least those she could decipher from the old-fashioned handwriting on many of the early ones, had documented decades of mysterious activities. Signal patterns. Midnight deliveries. Each entry raised more questions than it answered.

The sound of raised voices pulled her attention toward the courtyard.

"You can't just set up wherever you want." A man's deep voice carried clearly across the morning air. "There are rules about common areas."

"Clint, I'm not blocking anyone's access." A woman's voice was sharp with frustration. "I need the angle from this spot. The light hits the lighthouse differently here."

Emily set down her mug and leaned forward slightly, gazing out at the courtyard. Clint—*that was Winnie's nephew, right?*—stood with his arms crossed and his broad shoulders tense beneath a faded t-shirt. Facing him was a woman with shoulder-length brown hair pulled back in a practical ponytail. She wore muted gray clothing and had one hand resting protectively on an expensive-looking camera mounted on a tripod.

That must be Melissa Reeves, the photographer Winnie had mentioned.

Clint gestured toward the equipment. "The rules exist for a reason. You can't just claim space because it suits your artistic vision."

"My artistic vision?" Melissa's laugh held no humor. "That's rich coming from someone who's never created anything in his life."

Clint's jaw tightened. "I maintain this property. I protect it. That's creating something."

"You enforce arbitrary rules to feel important.

There's a difference." Melissa adjusted her camera's position slightly, as if to prove she wouldn't be moved by his protests.

"Those arbitrary rules keep this place running. Maybe if you spent less time hiding behind your lens and more time actually living in the community, you'd understand that."

The words hit their mark. Melissa's hand stilled on the camera. "At least I'm creating something," she shot back. "What are you doing besides following orders from your aunt and keeping everyone at arm's length?"

Emily remained still. The argument had shifted from property disputes to something far more personal, though she had no idea what history lay between them.

Before Clint could respond, the lighthouse keeper's quarters door opened.

Winnie emerged with the calm authority of someone accustomed to mediating conflicts. She wore a white shirt and a floral-patterned, flowing skirt, with her silver hair swept into a neat bun. Her gaze took in the scene with a single glance.

"Good morning. I see we're having a discussion about the courtyard space." Her voice carried clearly without being raised.

Clint turned toward his aunt. "She's set up her equipment in the common area again. Right on the pathway. We've talked about this."

"I need this specific angle." Melissa didn't look at Winnie, keeping her attention fixed on her camera. "The morning light creates shadows on the lighthouse that I can't capture from anywhere else."

Winnie walked closer, her steps measured and unhurried. She studied Melissa's setup for a long moment, then turned to examine the sight lines from each cottage.

"You're right that this angle offers a unique perspective," Winnie said finally. "And Clint is right that the courtyard is shared space."

Neither party looked satisfied with this even-handed assessment.

She turned to Clint. "But I don't think her equipment will really bother the other guests. Most of them don't really use the courtyard until later in the mornings anyway."

Melissa looked triumphantly at Clint.

Winnie then turned to Melissa and pointed toward a spot about six feet to the left. "That location gives you nearly the same angle while staying outside the direct pathway between cottages. You can set up there for your morning shots."

Melissa opened her mouth as if to argue, then closed it again. She gave a single, sharp nod. "That will work."

Winnie made it sound light, but Emily recognized the skill in what she'd just witnessed. Winnie had given each person something while requiring compromise from both. Neither had won completely, but neither had been dismissed either.

Melissa began breaking down her tripod without another word. Clint stood watching for a moment, his expression unreadable, before turning and walking toward the maintenance shed with deliberate steps.

Winnie remained in the courtyard, her gaze following first one, then the other. She turned and caught sight of Emily on her porch. The woman's expression shifted to something warmer, and she crossed the courtyard in quick steps.

"Good morning." Winnie paused at the bottom of Emily's porch steps. "I hope the excitement didn't disturb your coffee."

Emily glanced down at her mug. "It's gone cold anyway. That was some impressive mediation."

Winnie smiled. "Practice. I've been navigating lighthouse politics for more decades than I care to count."

"They seemed pretty worked up for a dispute about camera placement."

"It's never really about the camera placement." Winnie settled onto the porch step without waiting for an invitation. "May I?"

"Of course. Can I get you some coffee? Fair warning, mine's terrible, but I could make fresh."

"I'm fine, thank you. I had my fill this morning while reading the newspaper. Or trying to. The local paper has gotten distressingly thin. I remember when it was a proper newspaper with real investigative journalism."

"I noticed the Beacon has a historical column," Emily said. "Marty Fuller writes about the town's history. It even has a one hundred years ago and fifty years ago column."

"Marty runs Tides and Tales, the bookstore downtown. I think I mentioned that to you. Lovely man. Passionate about preserving local stories. You should visit his shop."

"I should drop by. I'd love to pick up a novel or two to read."

Emily glanced out to the courtyard and saw Melissa packing up her gear. She must have gotten the shots she wanted.

Winnie leaned back against the porch railing. "So, did you look at the journal more last night?"

The journal. Emily had almost forgotten about it in the drama of the morning argument. "I read through more of it. Your ancestor's documentation is somewhat vague. References to visitors who came and asked questions, but they were told nothing. Notes about sequences and confirmations, although I couldn't figure out all the entries."

"My grandfather was meticulous about his records. Sometimes too meticulous for his own good." Winnie stood, brushing invisible dust from her skirt. "Anyway, I should get back to my chores."

She started down the porch steps, then paused. "We're having our usual Friday gathering in the courtyard this evening. Nothing fancy. Just neighbors sharing a meal and conversation. You'd be welcome to join us."

"I'm not much for group socializing right now."

Winnie's face remained neutral. "I understand. But the invitation stands. Sometimes the best way to stop running is to stand still long enough to let people catch up to you."

She walked away before Emily could respond.

Emily sat for a long time after Winnie left, watching the morning light shift across the lighthouse's white walls. The structure itself seemed to pulse with secrets. How many people had stood where she sat now, watching the same lighthouse and wondering about the stories it held?

The sound of a door closing drew her attention. Melissa emerged from Captain's Watch Cottage carrying her camera bag. She wore a baseball cap pulled low. Without the tripod and equipment, she looked smaller somehow and more vulnerable.

Their eyes met across the courtyard.

For a moment, Emily thought Melissa might simply turn away. Instead, the photographer gave a small nod of acknowledgment before heading toward the path that led to the beach.

It wasn't much. It barely qualified as interaction. But something about the gesture felt significant.

She found herself standing and calling out before she'd consciously decided to do so. "The light's beautiful on the water this time of morning."

Melissa stopped walking. She turned back slowly, her expression guarded. "It is."

"I used to paint seascapes." She rose and crossed the distance between them. "Back when I painted. The morning light was always my favorite. That quality right after sunrise where everything looks both sharp and soft at the same time."

"Used to paint? You don't anymore?" Melissa frowned slightly.

"I'm taking a break." The euphemism felt ridiculous even as she said it. "An involuntary break, I guess."

Melissa's shoulders relaxed slightly. "I understand involuntary breaks." She adjusted the strap of her camera bag. "They're harder than the voluntary kind."

"Much harder." She paused, then decided to continue. "That's why I came here. Just to get some privacy. A break from… everything."

Melissa nodded as if she knew exactly how that felt.

They stood in silence for a moment.

Melissa looked at her like she wanted to say something more.

"What?" Emily asked.

"Well… the Friday gathering in the courtyard."

Melissa's gaze swept across the courtyard. "I usually skip them. Too many people, too much forced cheerfulness. But if you were thinking about going, it might be less awful with someone else there who also doesn't want to be."

"That's possibly the least enthusiastic invitation I've ever received."

Melissa's mouth lifted in something that might have been a smile. "I'm out of practice with people."

"Me too."

"So is that a yes?"

"Yes," she heard herself say. "It's a yes."

CHAPTER 7

Emily stood at her cottage window and watched Winnie arrange platters of food on the courtyard table. The warm glow of string lights illuminated the gathering space, making it look inviting and intimate. Too intimate.

She could still back out. No one would notice if she simply stayed inside with the curtains drawn and the lights off. They'd assume she was tired, busy, or simply not interested in socializing.

But Melissa had invited her. That awkward, tentative invitation had created an obligation she couldn't quite shake. She imagined Melissa arriving, looking for her, wondering if Emily had deliberately avoided her.

Emily took a deep breath and stepped outside into the warm evening air. The courtyard was more crowded than she'd expected. Several residents she recognized from the cottages mingled near the fire pit, while others were scattered throughout the space. Strangers. People from town, perhaps. This wasn't just a small gathering of cottage residents. This was a community event.

She crossed the courtyard slowly, acutely aware of how exposed she felt. Every face turned her direction felt like a spotlight, and every pause in conversation a potential judgment. She smoothed her hands down her shorts.

Then she spotted Melissa standing near the edge of the gathering, arms crossed, looking equally uncomfortable. Her camera was conspicuously absent. Relief flooded through her. At least she wasn't the only one who looked like she'd rather be anywhere else.

"You came," Emily said as she approached.

Melissa shifted her weight from foot to foot. "I said I would, though I'm already regretting it."

"Same." She managed a small smile. "How long do we have to stay before it's polite to leave?"

"I was thinking twenty minutes. Maybe thirty if Winnie corners us." Melissa's mouth twitched. "She has this way of making you want to please her. It's annoying."

"I've noticed." She glanced toward Winnie, who was laughing with a group near the fire pit. "She invited me with this look that said she knew I'd say no, but she was asking anyway."

"And here you are."

"Here I am."

They positioned themselves strategically near the food table, close enough to appear engaged but far enough from the fire pit to avoid being pulled into conversations. Emily picked up a plate she didn't want and studied the offerings with unnecessary concentration.

"Emily Shaw!" A cheerful voice cut through the ambient conversations. "I was hoping you'd be here."

Emily turned to find Sally Morris from the general store weaving through the crowd, carrying a covered dish. Her warm smile was genuine and unguarded. She reached the food table and set down her contribution before pulling Winnie into an easy embrace.

"Sally, you didn't have to bring anything." Winnie squeezed her friend's shoulders. "You know that."

"And miss showing off my new recipe? Not a chance. Besides, I've been coming to these gatherings for years. I know the rules." Sally's laugh was infectious.

This was what community looked like. What belonging felt like. She'd had that once in Chicago, before everything fell apart.

Sally turned her attention to Emily, her

expression softening. "How are you settling in? Finding everything you need?"

"Yes, thank you. The cottage is perfect." She managed what she hoped was a convincing smile.

"Starfish was always my favorite." Sally uncovered her dish, revealing what looked like a layered dip. "The last tenant stayed for nearly two years. Sweet woman, not a painter, but she loved that studio. Made it into a nice little sitting room." She turned to Melissa. "And how are you, dear?"

Melissa gave a noncommittal nod and a brief smile.

Winnie touched Sally's arm. "Come help me grab some more food from my cottage?"

Sally followed Winnie across the courtyard, leaving Emily and Melissa in their strategic corner once more. Emily picked up a cracker she didn't want and studied the crowd with renewed determination to appear engaged.

The door to Driftwood Cottage opened, and Clint emerged into the courtyard. He paused on his porch for a moment, surveying the gathering with the same expression Emily imagined she'd worn earlier. Reluctance radiated from every line of his posture.

He descended the steps and crossed to the food table as though he had a specific mission to complete before he could retreat. His gaze swept past Emily and Melissa with a brief nod that somehow managed to be both polite and dismissive.

Melissa stiffened beside her.

Clint grabbed a beer from the cooler and twisted off the cap. The movement was practiced and automatic. He took a long drink and swept his gaze across the courtyard, but he deliberately avoided looking at Melissa.

Sally returned with Winnie, both carrying additional trays. Clint positioned himself near Winnie.

Emily watched the way he angled his body slightly toward his aunt. Protective. Vigilant. Like he was standing guard rather than attending a social gathering. Winnie seemed oblivious to his hovering, or perhaps she'd simply grown accustomed to it over the years.

Sally pulled Clint into their conversation with the ease of someone who'd known him since childhood. She said something that made Winnie laugh, then touched Clint's arm with casual affection.

His shoulders dropped slightly. Not much, but enough that Emily noticed. He managed a small smile at whatever Sally had said, though his expression remained guarded.

Emily recognized that careful relaxation. The way you could appear engaged while maintaining emotional distance. The art of being present without actually being vulnerable. She'd perfected that skill herself over the past year.

Clint's gaze drifted toward their corner of the courtyard. Melissa studied her plate with sudden intensity. The tension between them was evident even from across the space.

Winnie clapped her hands together, the sound cutting through the various conversations scattered around the courtyard. "Everyone, gather around the fire pit for a moment."

The crowd shifted, forming a loose circle around the flames. Emily found herself pulled along with the movement, glad to feel Melissa beside her. She positioned herself slightly behind a taller man, hoping to maintain some anonymity in the group.

"I wanted to take a moment to welcome our newest resident." Winnie's warm gaze swept across the gathering before landing on Emily. "This is Emily, who's staying in Starfish Cottage."

Everyone turned toward her, and she managed a small wave that felt awkward and insufficient. A few people said, "Hi, Emily." Then the silence stretched just long enough to become uncomfortable.

Sally stepped forward, her smile as natural as breathing. "Emily, I've been meaning to ask. What brought you to Starlight Shores? We don't get many visitors this early in the season."

The question was innocent enough, but Emily's mind raced through possible answers. The truth was too complicated and too raw. She settled for something vague and hopefully believable. "I needed somewhere quiet to work. The lighthouse cottages seemed perfect."

"What kind of work do you do?" someone asked from across the circle.

"I'm an… artist." The words felt foreign on her tongue. Was she still an artist if she hadn't touched a brush in months?

Melissa's voice cut through her spiral of doubt. "Creative work requires solitude. You can't produce anything meaningful when you're constantly interrupted."

She glanced at her, surprised by the unexpected support. Melissa's expression remained indifferent, but she didn't look away.

Emily nodded. "That's true. Sometimes you need space to figure out what you're trying to say."

"Or remember why you wanted to say it in the first place," Melissa added quietly.

A moment of understanding passed between them.

Clint stood across the circle, his beer halfway to his mouth. He lowered it slowly, his gaze moving between Emily and Melissa with what looked like genuine interest rather than his usual guardedness.

The conversation shifted to safer topics. She heard snippets of discussion about the upcoming Harbor Festival, concerns about coastal erosion, and someone's recent fishing expedition. She let the voices wash over her, grateful to fade back into the crowd's periphery. The tension in her shoulders eased slightly as attention moved elsewhere.

Gradually, the gathering began to disperse. People drifted toward the food table for final helpings or stood in small clusters finishing conversations. The energy shifted from communal to intimate as the crowd broke into smaller, more natural groupings.

Sally wrapped Winnie in a warm embrace near the fire pit. "Same time next week?"

"Of course. Thank you for coming."

"Thank you for always making space for us." Sally pulled back, her eyes bright with affection. "This place has always been special because of you."

Emily watched the exchange from her position near the food table. That easy intimacy, the history between them evident in every gesture, was beautiful and painful all at once. She'd had friendships like that in Chicago. People she'd known for years, shared meals with, and trusted completely. Until the scandal hit, and those same people stopped returning her calls.

Sally waved goodbye to the remaining guests and headed toward the parking area. Others followed her lead, offering thanks to Winnie and friendly farewells to neighbors. The courtyard emptied in comfortable waves until only a handful of people remained.

Clint emerged from Driftwood Cottage with a large plastic bin and began collecting empty bottles and stray plates. His movements were efficient, like someone who'd done this routine countless times. Winnie joined him with another container, and they worked in tandem without needing to coordinate.

Winnie stacked paper plates. "You don't have to do that tonight. It can wait until morning."

"Takes five minutes now." Clint dumped bottles into the recycling bin with a satisfying clatter. "Besides, you know you'll be out here at dawn if I don't."

"I would not."

He smiled. "You absolutely would. Remember last month when you tried to move that table by yourself?"

Winnie waved a dismissive hand. "That table was lighter than it looked."

"It took three of us to carry it out here in the first place."

Their easy rapport was evident in every exchange. The way Clint anticipated what Winnie needed before she asked, and the way she accepted his help without making him feel like he was hovering. She felt a pang of longing for that kind of comfortable connection.

Melissa shifted beside her, drawing Emily's

attention back to their corner near the food table. They'd somehow ended up as the last non-family members in the courtyard, two women who'd spent the evening hiding in plain sight.

"Well," Melissa said after a moment, "that wasn't completely terrible."

Emily managed a small laugh. "High praise."

Melissa's expression softened slightly. "I mean it. I expected worse. Thanks for showing up. Made it easier having someone else who looked like they'd rather be anywhere else."

"Same." She glanced toward the fire pit, where Winnie and Clint continued their cleanup routine. "Though I think we might have been the only ones feeling that way."

"Probably. Everyone else seemed perfectly comfortable."

"Maybe they've had more practice."

Melissa picked up her empty water bottle. "Or maybe they're better at pretending. Either way, we survived."

"We did." She felt a slight shift. "Does it get easier? The gatherings, I mean."

"I don't know. I've only been here a few months, and I still feel like an outsider most of the time. I rarely come to these get-togethers." She paused. "But Winnie keeps inviting me anyway. I think she's either incredibly patient or incredibly stubborn."

"Both, probably."

"Definitely both." Melissa laughed. "I should go. Early morning shoot tomorrow if the light cooperates."

"Good luck with it."

Melissa nodded and headed toward Captain's Watch. Emily watched her go, then realized she was truly the last guest remaining. Winnie and Clint had finished their cleanup and were talking quietly near the fire pit, their voices too low to hear, but their body language was relaxed and familiar.

"Emily." Winnie's voice carried across the courtyard. "Don't you dare leave without taking some leftovers."

Emily crossed to where Winnie stood holding a container already packed with food. "You don't have to—"

"I absolutely do. Otherwise, Clint will eat nothing but Sally's dip for the next three days, and I refuse to enable that kind of behavior." Winnie pressed the container into Emily's hands. "Besides, I saw how little you ate tonight. You need proper fuel."

"Thank you." She accepted the offering. "And thank you for inviting me. It was... nice."

"You're welcome anytime. Same time next week?"

She hesitated only a moment before nodding. "Same time next week."

She walked back to Starfish Cottage with the

container of leftovers and paused at her door to glance back at the courtyard. Winnie and Clint still stood near the dying fire, their conversation unhurried and easy. The string lights emitted a warm glow over the space, making it look like something from a painting.

She'd survived her first community gathering. More than survived. She'd actually connected with Melissa, however tentatively. She'd managed polite conversation with Sally and hadn't completely fallen apart when Winnie introduced her to the group.

Maybe staying here wasn't impossible after all.

She unlocked her door and stepped inside, setting the container on the small kitchen counter. The cottage felt less like a hiding place than it had that morning. Less like a temporary refuge and more like... what? She wasn't ready to call it home. But maybe somewhere she could breathe for a while.

CHAPTER 8

Grant stared at his laptop screen, the glow harsh in the dim light of his apartment above the gallery. The article headline read: "Protégé or Predator? Emily Shaw and the Franklin Holloway Controversy." He'd been reading for over an hour now, clicking through links, following threads deeper into the story he'd only known in fragments.

He scrolled through another opinion piece, this one from an art critic who'd known Holloway personally. The writer defended Emily with passionate conviction.

He leaned back in his chair. The wood creaked beneath him.

He'd told himself this was research. Due diligence. The kind of thing any responsible community member would do when a stranger with a controversial past showed up in town. But the truth poked at him. He'd been searching for ammunition and evidence to support his initial wariness. Something concrete to justify the knot of unease that had settled in his gut the moment he'd recognized her at the farmer's market.

The problem was, the more he read, the less certain he became.

Some articles painted Emily as calculating and opportunistic. A woman who'd positioned herself perfectly to capitalize on a dying man's final creative burst. Others portrayed her as a scapegoat, someone caught in the crossfire of family disputes and art world politics that had nothing to do with her actual conduct.

The legal investigation had cleared her. That fact appeared in nearly every article, though some writers dismissed it with phrases like "technically cleared" or "no criminal charges filed," as if the absence of prosecution proved nothing about innocence.

Grant knew that dance. The way people could acknowledge your vindication while still treating you as guilty. The way a cleared name didn't necessarily clear a reputation.

He closed the laptop harder than necessary.

The apartment felt too small and too quiet. He stood and walked to the window overlooking Main

Street. The shops had closed hours ago. A few streetlights spilled yellow pools on the sidewalk.

His reflection stared back at him from the glass. When had he become this person? Someone who spent Friday evening alone in his apartment, researching a woman he barely knew, looking for reasons to justify his suspicion?

The pottery bowl. He'd left it on her doorstep like some kind of peace offering, then spent the walk home questioning his own motivations. Was it kindness or conscience? An apology for his rudeness or an attempt to maintain the town's reputation for hospitality?

He turned away from the window.

The truth was more complicated. He'd seen something in Emily's face at the farmer's market. When he'd spoken about her talent in the past tense, she'd flinched. Just for a moment. A flash of genuine hurt beneath her polished exterior before she'd raised those defensive walls higher.

He recognized that hurt. Knew it intimately.

He grabbed his keys from the counter. He needed to get out of this apartment and away from his own thoughts. The drive to his mother's house took less than five minutes. The porch light was on when he pulled into the driveway. She'd be reading in the living room. She always was.

His mother looked up from her book when he

let himself in through the front door. "Grant. This is a surprise."

"Restless." He crossed to the kitchen. "Thought I'd see if you had any of that pie left."

"Lemon meringue is in the fridge." Margaret Stone set her book aside. "Though I suspect you didn't drive over here at nine o'clock for pie."

He cut himself a slice and brought it to the living room. His mother waited, patient as always. She had a gift for silence and creating space that invited confession without demanding it.

"I met someone," he said finally.

His mother's eyebrows rose. "Oh?"

He stabbed his fork into the pie. "Not like that. A woman staying at the lighthouse. Emily Shaw."

"Winnie's new tenant. Sally mentioned her at book club. An artist, I heard."

"A controversial one. She was involved in a scandal in Chicago. Accusations of fraud and taking credit for her mentor's work."

"Was she guilty?"

"Legally? No. The investigation cleared her. But the art world wasn't so forgiving. Her reputation is destroyed. Her marriage ended. She lost her teaching position."

His mother studied him with those sharp eyes that had always seen too much. "And this concerns you because?"

"Because she's here now. In Starlight Shores."

He leaned forward. "What if she's looking for material? A new angle for her career? The lighthouse has historical significance. Winnie's family story. It could all become fodder for some exhibition or book that brings unwanted attention to the town."

"Could it? Or are you worried about something else?"

He stood and walked to the bookshelf where photos of his father lined the middle shelf. Jack Stone in his studio, brush in hand. Jack at a local art fair, surrounded by his coastal landscapes. Jack on the beach, collecting driftwood for his sculptures.

"Dad always said the hardest part wasn't creating the work. It was letting people see it. Letting them judge whether it mattered."

"Your father was a sensitive man. He felt things deeply. It made his art powerful, but it also made criticism painful."

He picked up a photo of his father at an exhibition opening. The smile looked strained around the edges. "He never got the recognition he deserved."

"He got the recognition that mattered to him." His mother stood and moved to his side. "He was respected here in this community. His work hangs in homes all over town. People treasure what he created."

"But he could have been more." The words

came out harder than Grant intended. "If he'd been willing to compromise, to play the game just a little bit, to market himself better."

"Is that what you think? That your father's integrity was a weakness?"

He set the photo down carefully. "I think the art world chews up people like him. People who care more about the work than the business. People who trust that talent and dedication will be enough."

"Like Emily Shaw?"

The question sat there between them. He turned to face his mother. "You don't know her story."

"Neither do you. But you've already decided what it is, haven't you? Decided she's someone who'll hurt this town the way you were hurt." She returned to her chair and picked up her book.

"I'm not—" He stopped. "This isn't about me."

"Isn't it? You came home seven years ago with wounds you've never discussed. You've built a good life here, Grant. A meaningful one. But you've also built walls. Very high ones."

"I'm protecting what matters."

His mother looked at him over her reading glasses. "Are you? Or are you protecting yourself from potential disappointment? There's a difference, sweetheart."

The silence stretched between them. Outside,

wind chimes sang in the breeze. His mother's clock ticked steadily on the mantel.

"She looked at my gallery," he finally said. "Emily. I saw her outside, watching through the window. She had this expression on her face like she was looking at something she'd lost. Something she wanted but couldn't have anymore."

"And that bothers you."

"It makes me wonder." He moved back to his chair and sat down heavily. "If she still paints. If she's given it up entirely or if she's just hiding. If she'll ever find the courage to try again after everything that happened."

His mother smiled. "You're describing yourself, you know."

He looked at his mother, this woman who'd raised him to see clearly, to think critically, and to question his own assumptions. "I run a gallery."

"You support other artists' work, which is admirable. But it's not the same as creating your own. When was the last time you made something, Grant? Something that mattered to you?"

He didn't answer. Couldn't.

"Your father used to say that sometimes we judge others most harshly for the things we fear in ourselves." His mother stood and kissed the top of his head. "I'm going to bed. Lock up when you leave."

He sat alone in his mother's living room for a

long time after she climbed the stairs. The house settled around him with familiar creaks and sighs. Through the window, he could see the dark shape of his father's studio at the back of the property. He hadn't been inside in months. Maybe longer.

His phone buzzed in his pocket. A text from Bryan, his friend who ran The Sandpiper: *Friday night and you're not at the bar. Everything okay?*

Grant typed back: *At Mom's. Needed pie.*

Ah, well, Margaret's pie beats out a beer any day.

He slipped the phone back in his pocket and stood. His mother's words echoed in his mind as he rinsed his plate in the kitchen sink. He locked the front door behind him and stood on the porch for a moment. The night air was cool, carrying the salt-sweet smell of the Gulf. Somewhere in the distance, he could hear the rhythmic crash of waves against the shore.

The lighthouse beam swept across the sky to the north. Steady. Reliable. Warning sailors away from danger.

Or guiding them home.

He climbed into his truck and told himself he'd drive straight back to his apartment. Get some sleep. Stop obsessing over a woman he barely knew and her reasons for coming to Starlight Shores.

But as he pulled out of the driveway, he found himself heading north instead of south. Toward the lighthouse. Just to drive past, he reasoned. Just to see if the lights were still on in Starfish Cottage. Just to check.

The justification felt thin even to him. But Grant made the turn anyway, following the coastal road as it curved toward the peninsula where the Lockhart Lighthouse had stood for more than a century. Guiding lost souls and marking dangerous waters.

Warning people away. Or inviting them closer.

He wasn't sure which anymore.

CHAPTER 9

Emily stood at the threshold of the studio, her hand resting on the doorframe. Three days had passed since she'd discovered the journal, three days of reading entries, making notes, and sketching architectural details. The easel waited in the corner, its blank canvas catching the morning light streaming through the north-facing windows.

She'd been avoiding it and telling herself she was just documenting the lighthouse's features for research purposes. She'd insisted the sketches were purely utilitarian and nothing more than a visual record to help solve the mystery of what the lighthouse keepers had really been doing all those years ago.

But the lie was wearing thin.

Emily pushed away from the doorframe and crossed to the worktable where her sketches lay scattered across the surface. She'd drawn the lighthouse from multiple angles, capturing the curve of the tower, the details of the keeper's cottage, and the way the gallery railing wrapped around the light chamber. Her pencil had found the rhythm of curved lines and shaded textures without conscious thought.

She picked up the sketch she'd made yesterday. The proportions were good. Better than good, actually. Her art historian training had kicked in, noting architectural details and structural relationships. The shading suggested more than she'd intended.

The way she'd shaded the lighthouse's base suggested not just form but weight, permanence, and endurance. The sketched clouds weren't mere background but active elements, their movement implied through careful cross-hatching. She'd even added the sea grass bending in an imagined breeze, though such details served no documentary purpose whatsoever.

She set the sketch down and turned to face the easel.

Just rough it out, she told herself. A quick study to see how the lighthouse's form translates to canvas. Nothing serious. Nothing that counts.

She selected a canvas from the stack that had been left in the studio. She picked a medium-sized one, not so large that it felt like a commitment, and not so small that it seemed precious. The familiarity of it felt both comforting and dangerous in her hands.

Before she could second-guess herself, she positioned the canvas on the easel and stepped back. Her heart was beating too fast. This was ridiculous. She'd painted hundreds of canvases over the years. Thousands, probably. Why did this one feel so monumental?

Because the last time you cared about your work, it destroyed you.

She shook her head, dismissing the thought. She wasn't going to care about this. It was just a study. Just a way to better understand the lighthouse's structure for the journal investigation.

She selected a charcoal pencil and approached the canvas.

The first line felt wrong. It was too tentative, too careful. She wiped it away with her thumb and started again. This time, she let her hand move with more confidence, blocking in the lighthouse's basic form with quick, assured strokes. The tower rose from the canvas as its cylindrical shape took form through the interplay of light and shadow.

She settled into the familiar rhythm of creation. The lighthouse emerged from white canvas like something surfacing from fog, its shape becoming more solid with each addition.

She lost track of time as she worked. She finally

unpacked from the box that she'd kept tucked away in the corner, and the charcoal sketch became the foundation for paint.

She found herself mixing colors on the palette without consciously deciding to do so. White with just a hint of yellow ochre for the lighthouse's sun-warmed walls. Cerulean blue deepened with ultramarine for the morning sky. The familiar smell of the paint surrounded her as she loaded her brush.

The first brushstroke of paint on canvas sent a shock through her. She paused, brush hovering in midair, waiting for the panic to hit. Waiting for the voice that would tell her she had no right to create anything and that she was a fraud.

But the voice didn't come. Instead, there was only the lighthouse taking shape beneath her brush, the morning light streaming through the studio windows, and the distant sound of waves against the shore.

She kept painting.

She added atmospheric details almost unconsciously. The way the morning light hit the lighthouse lens, creating a bright spot of reflected sun that she rendered with strokes of titanium white tinged with cadmium yellow. The texture of the tower's walls, where generations of salt air had weathered the surface into something both smooth and rough at once. The movement of sea grass in coastal breezes, each blade painted with quick, confident flicks of her brush.

These additions happened beyond her conscious control as her hand moved toward something more than documentation. The lighthouse wasn't just a structure anymore. It was a presence, a guardian, something that had stood watch over this coastline for more than a century while keeping secrets that even now remained partially hidden.

She stepped back from the canvas, surprised to find her shirt sleeves rolled up and a smear of paint across her forearm. How long had she been working? The light had shifted, and she glanced at the clock. Hours. She'd been painting for hours without noticing the passage of time.

The familiar rhythm of creating was both comforting and terrifying. This was how it used to be, before Franklin's death and his son's accusations. Before her ex-husband's betrayal. She would lose herself in the work and emerge hours later with paint in her hair and a canvas that felt alive in ways she couldn't quite explain.

She'd missed this. She'd missed this so much it physically hurt.

She whirled around at the sound of a knock at the studio side door. Winnie stood at the door, a tray in her hands. Emily crossed over and opened it.

"You're painting." Winnie stepped inside. Her

expression was warm but unreadable, her eyes taking in the canvas with obvious interest.

"I was just roughing out the lighthouse." She wiped her hands on a rag, suddenly self-conscious. "For reference. To help with understanding the journal entries."

"Of course." Winnie's tone suggested she didn't believe a word of it. She crossed to the worktable and set down the tray, which held a teapot, two cups, and a plate of what looked like lemon cookies. "I thought you might like some afternoon tea."

Afternoon. She still couldn't believe how long she'd been lost in her painting.

Winnie poured tea into both cups, then turned her attention to the sketches scattered across the table. She picked up one after another, examining them with the careful attention of someone who knew exactly what she was looking at.

Winnie held up a detailed sketch of the lighthouse's gallery railing. "These are remarkable. You've captured things I haven't thought about in years. The way the ironwork curves here, for instance. Most people don't notice that."

"It's an unusual design. The curve serves both aesthetic and functional purposes. It would help shed water while also creating visual interest."

"My great-grandfather had that railing custom-made. He was very particular about such details.

Said that beauty and purpose should always work together, never against each other."

She studied Winnie's face as the woman examined the sketches. There was something in her expression, a mixture of pride and sadness that suggested these architectural details carried personal meaning beyond their historical significance.

"This one is particularly interesting." Winnie held up a sketch showing the lighthouse's upper gallery, where Emily had noted unusual mounting brackets that seemed to serve no current purpose. "You have a good eye for anomalies."

"Those brackets…" Emily moved closer, pointing to the features she'd drawn. "They don't match the rest of the construction. They're newer, or at least they were added later. But they're positioned in a very specific pattern."

"Might be." Winnie's voice was noncommittal.

"But they're not there now?"

"No, they're not."

"Why were they removed?"

"The journal will tell you more than I can. The men in my family were careful about what they documented and what they kept only in their memory. But I suspect you're already discovering that."

Winnie moved to stand beside Emily, both of them now facing the canvas on the easel. The lighthouse rose from the painting, not quite finished but already possessing a life of its own. The morning light Emily had captured gave the structure a subtle quality, as though it existed between the real world and something more permanent.

"You're not just documenting. You're interpreting. Creating something new from what you see." Winnie's observation was gentle but pointed.

Emily's throat tightened. "I didn't mean to."

Winnie turned to look at her directly. "Why would you apologize for that? This is what artists do, isn't it? You take what exists and show others how to see it differently."

"I'm not sure I'm an artist anymore."

"Because someone accused you of being a thief?" Winnie's tone was sharp enough to make Emily flinch. "Or because you believed them?"

The words hit harder than she expected. She set down her teacup before she could drop it. "You know…"

"I know some of your past, yes."

"I didn't steal Franklin's work. I completed it, yes. He asked me to. He wanted those paintings finished, wanted his final vision realized even after he was gone. I thought I was honoring his legacy."

"And his son thought you were exploiting his father's death." Winnie's voice softened. "Two people can see the same situation and draw entirely different conclusions. That doesn't make one of them right and the other wrong. It just makes them human."

She turned back to the canvas, unable to meet Winnie's knowing gaze. "The art world decided Julian was right."

"The art world decided to protect itself. Controversy is messy. Easier to cast out one person than to ask complicated questions about collaboration and legacy and where one artist's vision ends and another's begins."

"You sound like you have experience with that."

"I've spent a lot of years watching people choose easy answers over difficult truths. It's one of humanity's most reliable patterns, I'm afraid. But it doesn't mean you have to accept their judgment as truth."

She wanted to believe that. Wanted to believe she could create again without fear of accusation and without judgment crushing every brushstroke. But the fear was still there, coiled tight in her chest like a living thing. "But what if I care about this again? What if I let myself care, and then it's taken away again?"

Winnie was quiet for a long moment. When she finally spoke, her voice carried the confidence of experience. "Then you'll survive it, just like you survived the last time. But not caring is its own kind of death. A slower one, perhaps, but no less final."

She let out a long, deep breath.

Winnie moved toward the door, then paused on the threshold. "The journal is waiting for you when you're ready. But so is this." She gestured toward the canvas. "Don't let fear make your decisions for you. You've already lost too much to it."

After Winnie left, she stood alone in the studio as shadows lengthened across the floor. The lighthouse painting caught the fading light, and for just a moment, she could see what it might become if she let herself finish it. Not a documentary sketch or a research tool, but a real painting. Something that mattered.

CHAPTER 10

Emily arrived at the beach just as the first hints of dawn touched the horizon. The air carried that particular stillness that came right before sunrise, when even the waves seemed to quiet. She'd woken at four-thirty, unable to sleep, her mind circling the lighthouse painting she'd worked on yesterday. The one Winnie had seen. The one that felt like both a beginning and an ending.

She'd decided sometime around five o'clock that hiding in her studio wasn't going to work anymore. If she was going to paint again—really paint, not just sketch under the guise of research—she needed to do it the way she used to. Out in the world. Facing what scared her.

The beach stretched empty in both directions, which was exactly what she needed. She planted her easel in the sand, adjusting the legs until they felt stable enough to withstand the gentle breeze coming off the water. Her hands moved through the familiar motions of setting up her palette, squeezing out paint in her preferred arrangement. Titanium white at the top, then her blues arranged from lightest to darkest. Her yellows and oranges. The earth tones she rarely used but always kept close.

She mixed a base color for the sky, combining cerulean blue with a touch of gray, then adding just a hint of violet. The color wasn't the cheerful blue of vacation postcards or the dramatic purple of storm paintings. It was the blue of uncertainty, of possibility that hadn't yet decided if it would materialize into something real or dissolve like morning mist.

The lighthouse stood silent against that tentative sky, catching the first rays of light. She loaded her brush and began with the basic shapes, blocking in the composition the way she'd done a thousand times before. But even as she worked on the technical aspects, her hand moved with a confidence she hadn't felt in years, laying down color with decisive strokes that came from somewhere deeper than conscious thought.

She lost herself in the rhythm of it. Brush to palette, mixing the exact shade she needed without overthinking. Brush to canvas, applying paint with just the right pressure. Back to palette, adjusting the color slightly.

The morning light shifted as she worked, and she shifted with it, adding touches of gold where the sun broke through the clouds. Not the bright, optimistic gold of hope, but more hesitant. A gold that suggested light was possible even if it hadn't fully arrived.

The sound of the waves provided a steady backdrop, punctuated by the occasional cry of gulls beginning their morning routines. Her feet had sunk slightly into the damp sand, anchoring her to the moment.

This was what she'd forgotten during those depositions and Daniel packing his things while she sat numbly on their couch. She'd forgotten that painting was a full-body experience, felt in her shoulders and her lower back.

She was mixing a darker blue for the shadows when she heard footsteps on the beach behind her. Her whole body tensed. She didn't turn around, hoping whoever it was would pass by without stopping.

Most people wouldn't interrupt someone who was clearly working. Most people would see the easel and the concentration and respect the obvious boundary.

But the footsteps slowed. Then stopped.

She could feel someone's presence just behind her left shoulder, close enough to see her canvas. Every instinct screamed at her to turn around, to step in front of the painting, and to hide what she'd been creating. But her hands were covered in paint, and moving would only draw more attention to her defensive reaction.

"I didn't expect to see you out here." Grant's voice. Of course, it was Grant. Because the universe apparently had a sense of humor about these things.

Her brush stopped mid-stroke. "I could say the same to you."

"I walk this beach most mornings." He moved slightly, coming into her peripheral vision but not directly in front of the easel. "Though I usually come earlier."

She didn't respond to that, focusing instead on cleaning her brush on the rag tied to her easel. Her heart pounded in a way that felt entirely too dramatic for the situation. He was just a man. This was just a painting. None of it mattered in any real sense. Except it did matter. It mattered more than she wanted to admit.

"You paint en plein air." His tone held a hint of respect, which somehow felt worse than suspicion.

"Sometimes." She loaded her brush with fresh paint, determined to continue working despite his presence. Maybe if she ignored him, he'd take the hint and leave.

"Not many painters work from life anymore. Easier to take a photo and work in a studio."

She heard a hint of genuine respect in his tone. "Easier isn't always better."

"No, it isn't." The agreement in his voice surprised her enough that she glanced over at him. He was studying her painting with the focused attention of someone who actually understood what he was seeing.

His expression had lost that wariness from their previous encounters, replaced by professional assessment, which was somehow worse. Professional assessment meant judgment. It meant comparison to other work, other artists. It meant all the things she'd been avoiding by locking herself in her cottage.

"I should go." She started to reach for her palette, preparing to pack everything up.

"Why?" The simple question stopped her.

"Because you're here."

"Am I stopping you from working?"

"You being here prevents me from being alone." She heard the defensive edge in her voice and hated it. "Which was kind of the point of coming out here at dawn."

Grant was quiet for a moment. When he spoke again, his voice was softer. "I'm sorry. I didn't mean to intrude on your work."

"But you did."

"I did." He didn't move to leave, though. "Your

technique is remarkable. The way you're handling the light—"

"Please don't." She cut him off, finally turning to face him directly. "I don't need your professional assessment or your compliments or whatever this is."

"I wasn't offering compliments. I was making an observation."

"Same thing."

"Not really." He shrugged. "A compliment is about making someone feel good. An observation is about recognizing what's actually there."

Emily wanted to argue with that distinction, but she couldn't quite find the words. She turned back to her painting, acutely aware of his presence just behind her. The wind picked up suddenly, strong enough that her canvas shook on the easel. She reached out to steady it, but Grant was faster. His hands caught the easel's legs, holding them firm against the gust. He moved with the easy familiarity of someone who'd steadied plenty of easels in his time, adjusting his grip to compensate for the uneven sand.

"You paint." The words came out before Emily could stop them.

Grant's hands tightened slightly on the easel legs. "Used to. I used to create…"

"Used to?"

"A long time ago." He released the easel once

the wind died down and stepped back. "Your canvas is still wet. You should probably get it inside before the breeze picks up again."

"I'm not finished."

"Then you should finish quickly." It was practical advice, the kind any experienced painter would give. But his tone suggested he was talking about more than just the painting. Emily studied his face, noting the tension in his jaw and the way his eyes had shifted from her work to the horizon.

"What did you create?" She didn't know why she asked. It was none of her business, and getting personal with Grant Stone seemed like a terrible idea on multiple levels.

"First, it was painting. But then I fell in love with sculpture using found objects from urban environments."

"But you don't create anymore?"

"No."

"Why not?"

His jaw tightened, and he looked past her toward the water. "Because I run a gallery instead. Someone needs to support other artists' work."

"That's not an answer."

"It's the only one I have." He took a step back, creating distance between them. "I should let you work. The light's changing."

He was right about the light. The sun had risen enough that the golden quality she'd been trying to capture had shifted, becoming harsher and more defined. She had maybe ten more minutes before she'd need to either commit to the new light or pack up.

She nodded in agreement, then he was walking away, his long strides carrying him down the beach toward town. She watched him go, and her mind raced with questions she had no right to ask. A sculptor who'd stopped creating. A gallery owner who handled easels with ease. A man who looked at her painting with recognition rather than judgment.

She turned back to her canvas, but the moment had broken. The absorbed flow she'd been in earlier felt impossibly distant now. She could see the painting with new eyes—Grant's eyes, maybe—and noticed the way her color choices betrayed her emotional state. All those muted blues and grays. The hesitant lighting. She was painting exactly how she felt. Anyone paying attention would see it.

The thought should have terrified her. A week ago, it would have. But standing there on the beach with her feet sunk into the sand and her hands covered in paint, she couldn't summon the fear she expected.

She mixed a new shade of blue, something slightly brighter than what she'd been using. She added it to the sky where the clouds were beginning to break apart, letting more light through.

She worked for another fifteen minutes before

the changing conditions forced her to stop. By then, she'd captured enough of the composition that she could finish the details in her studio if she wanted. But she liked it as it was. It was unfinished, uncertain, and honest in a way that felt both uncomfortable and necessary.

She packed up her supplies and walked back to her cottage slowly. Inside, she set the wet canvas on the drying rack in the studio, positioning it where she could see it from the doorway. The painting looked different in the softer interior light and more complete than it had seemed on the beach, but still obviously a work in progress.

A work in progress who'd just survived having someone see her in the middle of creating. Someone whose immediate response had been to protect her work rather than judge it.

She wasn't sure if surviving the encounter was good or just exhausting.

CHAPTER 11

Emily stood at her cottage door on Friday evening, contemplating the dozen excuses she could offer Winnie for skipping the Art Walk. Her hand hovered over the doorknob without turning it. But before she could retreat to her couch, a knock sounded.

"I know you're in there." Winnie's voice carried gentle amusement.

She took a breath before opening the door. "I was just—"

"Thinking of backing out?"

Winnie wore a coral cardigan and had traded her practical braid for a neat bun. Her small pearl earrings caught the porch light. She smiled patiently. "I understand the impulse. But hiding from the art community won't help you understand why the lighthouse matters to this town's cultural identity."

The argument was clever. She couldn't research the lighthouse's history in isolation, not really.

"I'm not exactly dressed for a night at a gallery." She gestured at her slacks and simple blouse.

"You look perfectly lovely. Besides, this is Starlight Shores, not Chicago. We value substance over style here."

The gentle rebuke hit its mark. She nodded, pulled the door closed behind her, and joined Winnie on the path toward town.

They walked in comfortable silence for several minutes. The lighthouse beam swept overhead at regular intervals, and salt air drifted from the nearby beach. Her shoulders gradually relaxed despite her nerves.

"I should warn you. People will be curious about you. It's natural in a small town." Winnie glanced at her as they reached the outskirts of downtown.

"I know. That's what worries me."

"Let them see who you are now, not what the internet says you were." Winnie patted her arm. "You're hardly the first person here with a complicated past."

She wanted to ask what Winnie meant, but they'd arrived at the beginning of the Art Walk, and the question dissolved as they joined the crowd. White booths lined both sides of the street, each one brimming with treasures crafted by local artisans. The air smelled of cedar shavings and fresh paint.

She spotted intricate wood carvings of lighthouses and old sea captains displayed alongside vibrant watercolor paintings of seascapes and mermaids.

One booth in particular caught her eye. It was staffed by a petite woman arranging a collection of handmade dresses for little girls, each piece a tiny work of art with delicate smocking and ribbon details that must have taken hours to perfect.

She turned to Winnie. "This is amazing. You have quite a turnout and lots of local talent."

"We do love our Art Walks."

They slowly made their way down the street until they arrived at Stone's Gallery. Light spilled from the large windows, and clusters of people already filled the space. She clenched her hands.

Winnie turned to her as they paused in the doorway. "Just breathe. You belong here as much as anyone."

The words were kind but felt unearned. She followed Winnie inside anyway.

The gallery was more impressive than Emily had realized from her previous glimpse through the windows. Polished concrete floors reflected track lighting positioned to showcase the artwork without creating glare. The space maintained its warehouse bones while serving its artistic purpose beautifully.

Grant stood near the entrance, speaking with an older couple. He wore dark jeans and a button-down shirt with the sleeves rolled to his forearms.

When he spotted Winnie and Emily, something flickered across his face. Surprise, maybe. Or wariness.

He excused himself from the couple and approached. "Winnie. Good to see you."

"I've brought Emily to experience her first Art Walk. She's been researching the lighthouse's history and needs to understand how it's shaped local artistic identity."

Grant's eyes shifted to Emily. She met his gaze directly, refusing to shrink despite her discomfort.

"Welcome to Stone's Gallery. We're featuring Gulf Coast landscape painters this month. Wine's on the table near the back."

"Thank you." She managed to sound calmer than she felt.

Winnie immediately spotted someone across the room and excused herself, leaving Emily alone with Grant. The silence stretched uncomfortably.

"I'll let you look around. Feel free to ask questions if you're curious about any pieces."

He moved away—or escaped—before she could respond. She stood awkwardly for a moment, then forced herself to approach the nearest wall of paintings.

The first piece showed the harbor at sunset, with all of its orange and purple drama. Competent but predictable. The kind of work tourists bought as souvenirs without really seeing the place underneath the pretty colors.

She moved to the next painting, which showed the same harbor from a different angle but with more attention to how light actually behaved on water.

"You have a good eye."

Emily turned to find a woman about her age with short blonde hair and paint-stained hands. "I'm sorry?"

"The way you looked at that first piece, then moved on. You knew immediately it wasn't worth your time." The woman smiled.

"I didn't mean to be rude."

"You weren't. You were honest. I'm Beth Ramsey. The second harbor painting is mine." She extended her hand.

Emily shook it, recognizing the name from the exhibition labels. "Emily Shaw."

"I know. Winnie mentioned you were staying at the lighthouse."

Of course, Winnie had laid the groundwork. She felt both grateful and exposed.

"Your painting shows real understanding of how coastal light works. The way you've handled the reflection on the water, especially where it breaks around the pilings. That's difficult to capture accurately."

Beth's eyes lit up. "Thank you. I've been trying

to get that particular quality for months. Most people just see water and boats."

They discussed technical approaches to painting reflections for several minutes. Emily found herself relaxing into the familiar language of artistic analysis. It was the part of her professional identity that felt safe and untainted.

Other artists gradually joined their conversation. Someone asked about Emily's background, and she mentioned teaching art history in Chicago without elaborating. When Grant came over and offered wine, she accepted gratefully.

The group exhibition varied widely in quality, which was typical of community shows. Some pieces felt like paint-by-numbers tourism, while others revealed genuine artistic vision. She studied a small canvas depicting the lighthouse through morning fog, noting how the artist had captured the structure's stability against atmospheric softness.

"That's one of Peter Martin's pieces." A voice spoke beside her. Emily turned to find an elderly woman with silver hair and bright eyes studying the same painting.

"It's a lovely painting. It shows the expert talent of the painter."

The woman smiled. "Ah, that would be my late husband, Peter. Though that one's from forty years ago. Peter and I both painted the lighthouse regularly. It changes character depending on the weather and season. I'm Charlene, by the way."

"The architectural details are fascinating." Emily pointed to the painting's background, where the structure's base showed more clearly than it appeared today. "The lighthouse looks slightly different now."

"It does. Peter documented those changes over the years. He was meticulous about accuracy. Used to say buildings tell stories if you know how to read them."

"Did he leave records of what he observed?"

"Not specifically. Though he always suspected the lighthouse had served purposes beyond navigation."

"What made him think so?"

"Architectural anomalies he noticed over decades of painting the structure. Modifications that didn't match official records. He had an eye for details like that." Charlene shrugged. "Well, I should go mingle a bit. It was nice to meet you."

As the older woman moved on to greet other attendees, Emily realized she'd been fully engaged in conversation for the first time in months without worrying about judgment or exposure.

She continued through the gallery, studying the various interpretations of the coastal landscape. Some artists focused on the dramatic and emphasized storms and crashing waves. Others captured quiet moments of morning light or intimate beach scenes. The range of vision was remarkable and solid proof that even a small geographic area could inspire infinite artistic responses.

Grant appeared at her elbow as she examined a painting of the lighthouse during a storm. "What do you think?"

She considered the question seriously. The painting was technically proficient but emotionally hollow, all sound and fury without genuine feeling. "It's well executed. But it feels like the artist is painting the idea of a storm rather than the actual experience of weather."

"That's diplomatically put." His lips curved into a slight smile.

"You asked what I think. I assume you want honest feedback, not polite lies."

"I do. The artist is talented but young. Still learning to trust personal observation over photographic reference."

They stood in silence, both looking at the painting. She was vividly aware of his presence beside her and the way he unconsciously assessed the artwork's composition and the gallery's traffic flow simultaneously.

He turned to her. "Beth told me you gave her excellent technical advice about painting water reflections. She's been struggling with that particular challenge."

"She has good instincts. She just needs to trust them more."

"That seems to be a common problem." His tone suggested he wasn't just talking about Beth.

Emily turned to face him directly. "Why did you really come over to talk to me? You've been avoiding me most of the evening."

He looked startled by her directness, then rueful. "Fair observation. I've been wanting to apologize to you. Should have when I saw you painting on the beach. I wanted to apologize for my rudeness when I saw you at the farmer's market. I made assumptions I shouldn't have."

"You mean you assumed I was a fraud who exploited my dying mentor? You wouldn't be the first person to believe that."

He winced. "I did read about the controversy. But watching you tonight and seeing how you engage with art and artists, I realize the situation must have been more complicated than the headlines suggested."

"It was. But I don't expect you to take my word for it. Most people prefer the dramatic version anyway."

"I'm trying not to be most people." His gaze was earnest.

She broke eye contact first, turning back to the

storm painting. "Your gallery is impressive. You've created something special here."

"Thank you. That means a lot coming from someone with your background."

"My tarnished background, you mean."

"Your professional background. Teaching art history at a prestigious university, curating for the museum, and showing in some well-known galleries. That doesn't disappear because of a scandal."

She blinked, surprised he'd researched her career beyond the controversy. "Most people only know about the accusations."

"I'm not most people," he repeated quietly.

Before she could respond, Winnie appeared, and the moment between Emily and Grant dissolved. He excused himself to greet new arrivals.

The Art Walk continued for another hour. Emily found herself drawn into multiple conversations about artistic technique, local history, and the lighthouse's significance to the community's identity.

Everything was fine until one woman came up to her and frowned. "Don't I know you from somewhere?"

She smiled weakly. "I don't think so."

"Maybe from back in Chicago?"

Her heart pounded, waiting for the recognition.

"Guess not." The woman turned and walked over to another display.

She let out a long breath. She thought coming

all the way to a small town in Florida would provide her with a safe space where no one would recognize her. But Grant had. At least Julian had no idea where she was. That was the most important thing. At least he didn't know yet…

When the crowd finally thinned, they headed back to the lighthouse. The cool night air felt refreshing after the crowded space.

"You did well tonight. I watched you come alive during those conversations about art." Winnie smiled at her as they walked under the glow of a streetlamp.

"It felt good to talk about painting again without feeling like a pariah. I'd forgotten what that was like."

"You're not a pariah here. You're a researcher, an artist, and someone who understands how to really see things."

She wanted to believe it. For the first time since the scandal broke, she'd spent an evening as a person rather than a cautionary tale. People had listened to her opinions, valued her expertise, and engaged with her ideas without hidden judgment lurking behind every word.

But Grant's wariness still troubled her. She'd felt it despite his apology and seen it in how he'd positioned himself throughout the evening. He was watching her and trying to decide something.

Whether she was trustworthy, probably.

Whether she belonged in his carefully curated artistic community.

The lighthouse beam swept overhead as they approached the property. She counted the rhythm automatically now, finding comfort in its predictability.

"Grant is a good man. But he's been hurt. He has his own reasons for being careful about who he lets close," Winnie said suddenly.

She glanced at Winnie, wondering how much she actually saw. Probably everything. "I'm not trying to get close to anyone. I'm just trying to exist without people assuming the worst about me."

"That's a start. But eventually, you might want more than just existence."

Emily pushed through the weathered door of The Sandpiper, and the scent of grilled fish and fried food surrounded her. The restaurant hummed with energy. Conversations layered over each other while silverware clinked against plates.

She'd told herself this was just dinner. A practical choice after a long day of painting. Nothing to do with avoiding another evening alone with her thoughts and the lighthouse journal.

The hostess gestured toward the bar. "Might be a twenty-minute wait for a table. Or you can eat at the bar."

"Bar would be fine." She slid onto a barstool near the end, grateful for the position that let her observe without being observed. Old habits.

The man tending the bar smiled. "Welcome to

The Sandpiper. Don't think I've seen you in here before."

"I'm staying at the cottages at the lighthouse."

"Ah, the artist." He smiled again. "I'm Bryan. My family runs The Sandpiper. What can I get you?"

"It's nice to meet you. I'll have whatever local beer you'd recommend."

"Seaside Wheat Beer, it is. Brewed right here in Starlight Shores."

She accepted the amber bottle and took a tentative sip. Not bad. Actually quite good. She let her gaze wander across the restaurant's interior. Exposed beams overhead. Vintage photographs of fishing boats and harbor scenes covered the walls. Through the large windows, the Gulf stretched toward the darkening horizon.

A burst of laughter drew her attention to a large corner booth where a group of locals gathered. Winnie's friend, Sally, sat with them, and several other familiar faces from the Art Walk filled the booth.

"I'm telling you, Mayor West has already made up her mind." A man's voice carried above the others. "The zoning commission meeting is just a formality."

"Mayor West wouldn't sell us out like that." Sally's tone held more hope than conviction.

"She's not selling anyone out. She's being

practical." This came from an older man with calloused hands wrapped around a beer bottle. "The town needs the tax revenue. We all know it."

Emily shifted slightly, angling herself to hear better without appearing obvious.

"At what cost, though?" A younger woman leaned forward. "If Oceanside Development gets that waterfront property, they'll turn the whole Gulf front into another Clearwater Beach. High-rises and chain restaurants."

Bryan appeared at Emily's elbow. "Ready to order?"

"Just a few more minutes. Just enjoying my beer."

He nodded and moved away.

"Grant's got the right idea," Sally said again. "Fight to keep what makes this place special. Once it's gone, it's gone."

"Grant can afford principles. His gallery doesn't depend on tourist dollars the way my charter business does." The older man's tone wasn't unkind, just matter-of-fact.

The younger woman swirled her wine glass. "Actually, his gallery barely breaks even. My cousin does his bookkeeping. He pours every profit back into supporting local artists."

Emily's hand tightened slightly on her beer bottle.

"That's because he's still trying to prove

something." Another voice joined in. "Still trying to show he's not like those New York gallery people who betrayed him."

They all nodded.

Emily frowned. *What happened in New York?*

"Well, at least he came back home. Opened Stone's Gallery in that old warehouse nobody else wanted. Been fighting to preserve the town's character ever since."

"Because he gets it. He knows what it's like to lose something to people who only see dollar signs." Sally's voice held fierce loyalty.

"The resort development isn't just about money, though." The younger woman glanced around. "It's about survival. Half the businesses on Main Street barely made it through last year."

"Which is exactly what Oceanside is counting on. Desperation makes people compromise." Sally straightened.

The conversation shifted to more speculation about the mayor and where she stood on all of this.

Emily turned back to the bar and studied her beer bottle's label, gently peeling back the edge of it. Grant had been betrayed. No wonder he'd looked at her with such suspicion at the farmer's market. No wonder he'd asked what brought her to Starlight Shores with that particular edge in his voice. She was probably a walking reminder of everything he'd run from.

Bryan reappeared. "Your table's ready if you'd like. Or you can order here at the bar."

"Here's fine." She accepted the menu without really seeing it and ordered automatically. Grilled grouper sandwich and coleslaw. Safe choices.

While she waited, her mind circled back to Grant and the gallery that barely broke even. To his fight against development pressure that threatened the town's authenticity. To his careful support of local artists.

He was trying to protect something. Trying to preserve what mattered against forces that only saw commercial potential. She understood that impulse. She'd spent months protecting what remained of her own reputation, guarding against anyone who might weaponize her past mistakes or misunderstand her intentions.

But protection became stifling eventually. She was learning that slowly.

Her food arrived, and she ate while half-listening to conversations flowing around her. The locals moved from development concerns to speculation about summer tourist projections to someone's daughter's wedding plans. Normal life. Community life. The kind of interconnected existence she'd lost when scandal had isolated her.

She'd had this once in Chicago, with a network of colleagues and friends who understood her references and shared her passions. People who knew her well enough to read her moods and offer support without being asked.

Daniel's betrayal had been devastating, but losing her professional community had been equally disastrous in its own way. All those carefully cultivated relationships had evaporated overnight when accusations started flying.

Through the window, Emily could just make out the lighthouse beam beginning its sweep across the darkening sky. Reliable. Constant. Present. Winnie had said the lighthouse attracted people who needed healing and those searching for something they couldn't name. Maybe Grant Stone had been one of those people when he returned home. Maybe he'd come home wounded and determined to create something authentic in a world that had shown him its ugliest face.

And now here she was, carrying her own wounds and complicated history. No wonder he kept his distance.

She paid her bill and stepped out into the humid evening air. The harbor stretched before her. Boat masts swayed gently. Water lapped against wooden pilings. Somewhere, a gull cried out.

The gallery sat a few blocks down, its windows dark for the evening. She found herself walking toward it anyway. She stopped across the street and studied the building. The warehouse conversion showcased thoughtful design with large windows, clean lines, and respect for the original structure's character. A man who built something like this understood preservation and the difference between honoring the past and being trapped by it.

She turned toward home. She'd learned something tonight that mattered. Grant Stone wasn't just some suspicious local protecting his territory. He was someone who understood loss. Someone who'd been betrayed by the same world that had betrayed her. He poured every profit back into supporting local artists, still trying to prove something. That knowledge changed things.

CHAPTER 13

The pottery mug felt solid in Emily's hands. She'd made coffee in the little kitchen, finding comfort in the morning routine she'd established over the past few weeks. The bowl Grant had left still rested on the windowsill, filled with her beach stone and shell collection. Small, simple things that anchored her somehow.

She finished her coffee and got dressed. The sun wasn't fully up yet. There was just that soft pre-dawn light that painters loved.

The beach called to her. It always did these days. She stepped out onto the porch and headed down the path toward the beach. The sand was cool beneath her bare feet. She carried nothing. No sketchbook today. No agenda. Just the water and maybe some peace.

But someone was already there. Melissa stood

near the water's edge with her camera equipment arranged around her like sentries. She was crouched low, angling a shot toward the lighthouse from an unusual perspective. The tripod looked complicated. Professional. The kind of setup that took time and intention.

She hesitated. Melissa had been friendly enough at the gathering. They'd bonded over their shared discomfort with crowds. But that didn't mean she wanted company now. Some people needed solitude for their work. She started to turn back.

"You can stay." Melissa's voice carried across the sand. She didn't look up from her camera. "Or I won't be offended if you want to just walk past and have your privacy. I'm just documenting."

Emily walked closer instead. Something in Melissa's tone made it clear she wasn't merely being polite. She genuinely didn't mind either way.

"Documenting?" She kept her distance from the equipment, knowing how particular photographers could be about their setups.

"The lighthouse." Melissa adjusted something on her camera. "Architectural details. The way the light hits certain modifications in the structure. There are additions and changes that aren't in the original blueprints. At least not the ones available at the historical society."

Another person interested in the lighthouse's history.

"What kind of changes?" The art historian in her couldn't help asking.

"Windows that don't match. Modifications to the gallery deck. A door on the north side that's been there longer than it should be based on the construction date." Melissa finally looked up. "I've done this for a while. You develop an eye for what doesn't fit."

"You taking these photos for a project?"

Melissa straightened and stretched her back. "No, just for the record. So many of these places get torn down, renovated beyond recognition, or they just deteriorate until the story they could tell disappears. I document them before that happens."

She understood that impulse and the need to preserve something before it vanished. She'd felt it when completing Franklin's final works, though that preservation had cost her everything.

"I could hold something for you." The offer came before Emily could think better of it. "If you need an extra hand."

Melissa considered her for a moment. Not suspicious exactly. Just careful. "I want to move closer and get the sea oats next to the base of the lighthouse. If you could stand and hold that panel steady while I get this angle, that would help."

They moved closer to the lighthouse, and she stood where Melissa indicated. The panel was lighter than it looked. She held it at the angle Melissa demonstrated.

"There." Melissa took several shots. "Can you tilt it a bit more toward the water?"

She adjusted it, and they worked in comfortable silence. The beach was completely empty except for them. Even the gulls were quiet this early. There was just the sound of the waves and the occasional click of Melissa's camera.

"You paint it." Melissa didn't phrase it as a question. "The lighthouse."

"I've tried a few times. It's harder than it looks to capture."

"Everything worth capturing is." Melissa moved her tripod slightly. "Hold that angle for just a minute more."

She held still.

"Got it. Thanks. That made a real difference."

"What will you do with the photographs?" Emily handed back the reflector panel.

Melissa began packing her equipment. "Keep them. Create an archive. Maybe eventually a book about Gulf Coast architecture. Structures that tell stories about the communities that built them."

"The lighthouse definitely tells a story." She thought about Winnie's journal and the hints about hidden purposes. "More than one, probably."

"Most old buildings do. People think architecture is just about function. Keeping the rain out. But it's really about intention. Every change was a choice. Shows you what mattered to them."

She understood that concept. She'd studied enough art history to know that context mattered. That the story behind a work could be as important as the work itself. "You approach it like a historian."

"Photography taught me to look deeper. To see what's actually there instead of what I expect to be there. Though I haven't been very good at that lately."

"I haven't been very good at painting lately." She surprised herself by responding with equal honesty. "Or I hadn't been until I came here."

Melissa looked up at the lighthouse. "It helps. The lighthouse helps. There's something about it and the way it just stands there, being exactly what it is. No apologies. No explanations. Just doing its job century after century."

"Winnie says it attracts people who need that." She glanced back toward the keeper's cottage. "People who need to figure things out."

"She told you that?"

"In slightly more poetic terms." She smiled despite herself. "But yes."

Melissa finished packing. She shouldered her equipment bag and picked up the tripod. "I should get this back before the sun gets too high. The light will be wrong for what I'm doing."

"Thank you for letting me help." Emily meant

it. The simple act of holding something steady while someone else worked had felt good. Useful. A small contribution to something that mattered.

"Thank you for not asking about my camera settings or telling me I should try a different angle." Melissa smiled. "Most people can't resist offering advice."

"I know what that's like, having everyone assume they know better than you what you should be doing."

"Yeah. I figured you would."

They walked back toward the cottages together. The sun had broken fully over the horizon now. The lighthouse stood clear and solid in the morning light.

"If you want to look at the photographs sometime, let me know." Melissa paused at the path that branched toward her cottage. "I've got documentation going back several weeks. The changes are subtle, but they're there."

"I'd like that. I've been researching the lighthouse's history and trying to piece together why certain things are the way they are."

"We should compare notes then. Between your research and my photographs, we might actually figure some things out."

Emily watched her walk away. Another small connection made. The fear that had paralyzed her for months felt smaller today and a bit more manageable.

CHAPTER 14

Emily stood in the center of the studio with morning light streaming through the north-facing windows. She had been working for three hours straight. Her back ached, and her fingers were stiff, but she couldn't stop.

The canvas before her showed the lighthouse keeper's quarters from decades past, a lived-in space where real people made impossible choices. She had used the journal entries as her guide. The details mattered. The brass oil lamp was positioned just so on the desk. The nautical charts rolled in their leather case. The worn armchair angled toward windows that offered both harbor views and constant vigilance.

But the painting wasn't just documentation. Her approach had shifted as the work progressed. The lighthouse keeper's desk dominated the composition with its layers of maps, logbooks, and a half-written letter that would never reveal its contents.

She had painted the letter with deliberate ambiguity. Viewers would wonder what words lay hidden beneath the keeper's hand. What truths were being recorded or concealed?

This is what painting should feel like. Not performing. Not proving. Just seeing something true and finding a way to show it.

Her previous work, even before the scandal, had been different. Technically accomplished but emotionally restrained. She had painted to earn approval from professors, galleries, and eventually her mentor, Franklin.

Even the paintings she had completed for Franklin before his death had been exercises in replication. She had tried to channel his voice, his vision, and his distinctive approach to light and composition. She had told herself it was respectful collaboration. Now she wondered if she had been hiding inside his reputation all along.

This painting was hers alone. Raw and honest in ways that made her feel exposed.

She stepped back to assess the work with a critical eye. The composition held together. The architectural details read as authentic. But the emotional undertones carried the piece beyond mere illustration. The room felt inhabited by people carrying the burden of protecting something larger than themselves.

Emily understood that better now. Winnie carried it. Clint carried it. Even Grant carried some version of it, protecting his carefully built sanctuary from a world that had already wounded him once.

She mixed more color on her palette. The letter on the desk needed refinement. She wanted the viewer to lean in, to wonder, and to actually feel the keeper's hesitation about what should be written versus what could safely be revealed.

The brush moved across the canvas with a confidence she hadn't felt in years. Every stroke felt inevitable. Necessary. True.

She was so absorbed in the work that Winnie's soft knock startled her.

"Come in." Emily set down her brush and turned.

Winnie entered with her characteristic quiet grace. She carried no tea this time and no excuse for the interruption.

"I don't mean to disturb you. I just wondered if you might want some company."

Emily hesitated. Part of her wanted to protect this private space. But another part, the part that was slowly relearning connection, recognized the invitation for what it was.

"I'm at a good stopping point. Would you like to

see what I've been working on?" She wiped her hands on a paint-stained towel.

"Only if you're comfortable sharing."

She moved aside to give Winnie a clear view. Her heart hammered with unexpected nervousness. This painting mattered more than anything she'd created in years. Maybe ever. And Winnie's opinion mattered more than an ordinary critique.

Winnie went very still. She studied the canvas in complete silence while Emily counted her own heartbeats. Five. Ten. Twenty.

Then Emily saw the tears.

They formed slowly in Winnie's eyes and spilled over without drama. Winnie didn't brush them away. She simply let them fall as she continued examining every detail of the painting.

"You painted my grandfather's study. I haven't seen this room since I was a child. After my grandfather died, my father couldn't really bear to go into the study. He eventually knocked down a wall and made the family room larger, and all remnants of the study disappeared. He said the study had served its purpose." Her voice was thick with emotion.

"I didn't know. I just followed the journal entries and some sketches in the journal and tried to imagine what the space might have looked like based on the details he mentioned. The lamp, the charts, the—"

"The chair." Winnie pointed with a trembling hand. "That chair faced the windows at exactly that angle. He could watch the harbor and see the lighthouse beacon both. He said a keeper should never fully relax. Should always maintain awareness."

Winnie stepped closer to the canvas. "He was writing to my grandmother the night I was born. I found that letter years later in her things. He wrote about duty and love and the choices we make to protect the people who depend on us. You've captured the true reality here, Emily. Not just what the room looked like, but what it felt like to be him. To carry those responsibilities."

"I kept thinking about a safe harbor while I painted." Emily slowly let out a long breath. "About what it means to be the keeper of something larger than yourself. To maintain a light that guides others while maybe feeling lost yourself."

"Yes. That's exactly right. The lighthouse was always both refuge and burden. My great-grandfather understood that. Then my grandfather and my father. I understand it now."

Winnie turned to face Emily directly. Her expression held complicated layers of grief and recognition. "You have a gift, Emily. Not just technical skill, though you clearly have that. But the ability to see beneath surfaces. To understand what people were feeling, not just what they were doing."

Emily felt her own eyes sting. Praise felt dangerous after so many months of accusation. But Winnie's words didn't feel like flattery. They felt like real admiration.

"I lost that for a while," she admitted. "Or maybe I never fully trusted it before. I was always trying to paint the right way. To demonstrate my understanding of artistic tradition and historical context. To prove I belonged in rooms where people discussed art seriously."

"And now?"

She looked back at the canvas. The lighthouse keeper's study gazed back at her with all its accumulated secrets. "Now I'm just trying to see what's true. To paint what I actually feel instead of what I think I should feel." She paused and turned to Winnie. "It's terrifying."

Winnie smiled and wiped away the last of her tears. "Yes. The truth usually is. But it's also the only thing worth painting. Or living, for that matter."

They stood in silence for a few moments, just looking at the canvas. Finally, Winnie said, "Thank you for seeing my grandfather clearly. For honoring what he was trying to do. This painting captures what I've been trying to explain to people for years. The lighthouse was never just about navigation. It was about creating a sanctuary, a safe haven. About being the steady force when everything else felt uncertain."

She nodded. She couldn't trust her voice yet.

Winnie moved toward the door but paused on the threshold. "I hope you'll consider showing this work, Emily. Not to prove anything to the people who judged you. But because this is the kind of truth that deserves to be seen."

Emily stood alone with the painting. The morning light had shifted during Winnie's visit. The canvas looked different now. More complete somehow. More real.

But she wasn't ready to show her work. Not now. Probably not ever.

She picked up her brush again. But instead of continuing the detail work, she simply added her initials in the lower right corner.

E.B. Simple and hers.

CHAPTER 15

G rant hadn't seen Emily in days, even though he'd faithfully taken a morning walk past the lighthouse each day. Today, he spotted Emily on the beach before she noticed him. She stood at her easel with her back to the path, her attention completely absorbed by the canvas. The morning light caught in her auburn hair as the wind pulled strands loose from her bun.

He should keep walking. His route took him past this stretch of beach most mornings, but he could easily cut inland through the dunes. Give her the space she clearly wanted. That would be the smart choice.

His feet kept moving toward her anyway.

She'd made adjustments since their last encounter. The easel had sandbags weighted at the base, and she'd angled it to use the wind rather than fight against it. A beach umbrella stood planted nearby, positioned to diffuse the harsh morning sun without blocking her view. She wore a wide-brimmed hat and loose layers that could be shed or added as the temperature shifted.

Someone who was planning to paint here regularly. Not a tourist chasing a single sunrise.

The observation unsettled him more than it should have.

"Mind if I look?"

Emily startled slightly but didn't turn around. Her brush paused mid-stroke. "Go ahead."

He moved to where he could see the canvas without crowding her workspace. The painting showed the lighthouse from a different angle than her previous work. Early morning light washed across the keeper's quarters, turning the walls golden while the lighthouse tower remained in shadow. She'd captured the way dawn arrived in stages here, illuminating surfaces gradually rather than all at once.

The technical skill impressed him. She knew what she was doing with a brush. She understood how to layer color to create depth, how to suggest texture without overworking the surface. The composition balanced structure and atmosphere in ways that required both training and intuition.

But that wasn't what held his attention. Something in the way she'd painted the light made the scene feel inhabited. Lived in. The windows of the keeper's quarters reflected the sky, but they also suggested someone inside looking out. Someone waiting for something or watching over something precious.

"You're spending real time with it."

"With what?" She glanced at him briefly before returning to her canvas.

"The light. The way it changes through the morning. This isn't observation from a single session. You've been watching it for days."

She added a stroke of pale blue to one of the windows. "Is that a criticism?"

He heard the defensiveness in her question and tried again. "No, it's an observation. Most painters show up, capture the moment they see, and leave. You're studying it. Building understanding over time."

Her grip loosened on her brush. "The light's different every morning. Different clouds, different humidity, and a different angle of the sun. I kept getting it wrong. Too stark or too soft. Finally realized I needed to stop trying to paint one perfect morning and start painting the truth of all of them."

He'd hit that wall too. Every artist did eventually. You had to let go of trying to capture what you saw and start expressing what you understood.

Miranda had never made that transition. Her paintings remained technically polished but emotionally hollow. She'd perfected her style early and never pushed past it, never risked failing in pursuit of something deeper. He'd admired her confidence at first. Only later did he recognize it as a limitation rather than a strength.

"The way you've painted the keeper's quarters," he said carefully, "it feels like someone's home, not a historical building."

"It is someone's home. Winnie lives there. Has her whole life. It's not history to her. It's just a regular morning."

She'd done what most artists spent years looking for and found the reality beneath the picturesque surface. Tourists painted the lighthouse as an object. Emily was painting it as a place where people built lives.

She stepped back from her easel and studied the canvas with narrowed eyes. "The shadow on the lighthouse's base is wrong. Too uniform. There's a texture to the brickwork that breaks up the darkness differently."

He moved slightly closer, seeing what she meant. "The mortar lines. They're recessed enough to catch indirect light even when the main surface is in shadow. Creates a subtle pattern."

"Yes." She looked at him directly for the first

time since he'd arrived. "You've painted it. The lighthouse, I mean."

"A long time ago." He shoved his hands in his pockets. "Before I opened the gallery."

"Why'd you stop?"

The question was casual, but her eyes held genuine curiosity. Not the prying kind that wanted gossip, but the artist kind that recognized shared experience.

"Got busy with other things. The gallery takes up a lot of time." The half-truth felt shallow.

She nodded slowly but didn't quite look like she believed him. She turned back to her canvas and began mixing a darker blue. "I didn't paint for over a year. Kept telling myself I was too busy dealing with legal issues. Too stressed to focus. Waiting for the right time."

She added the new color to the tower's shadow, using a dry brush to create the texture she'd described. "Finally realized I was just afraid. Easier to not try than to try and confirm I'd lost it."

The honesty in her admission surprised him. "Did you? Lose it?"

"I don't know yet. Some days this feels like remembering something I used to know. Other days, it feels like learning from scratch. Maybe it's both."

The vulnerability in her voice undermined every assumption he'd made about her. This wasn't someone exploiting a scandal for attention. This was an artist trying to find her way back to work that mattered. He recognized that struggle because he'd been avoiding it for seven years.

She glanced at him. "Your painting before. The work you did. Was it good?"

"I thought so." He surprised himself by answering honestly. "I was doing sculptures of found objects, mostly urban materials, trying to show how cities grow and change through the debris they leave behind."

"Past tense."

He looked out at the water instead of at her. "Yeah, things got complicated. When I came back here, I told myself I'd get back to it eventually. Just needed to get the gallery established first."

"How long has it been established?"

"Six years."

She made a soft sound that might have been understanding or acknowledgment. She cleaned her brush and reached for a different color. "People kept telling me I'd paint again when I was ready, like readiness was something that would just happen if I waited long enough. I finally figured out I'd never feel ready. I just had to start anyway and let ready catch up."

The words felt aimed at him, though her focus stayed on her canvas. He watched her add warm gold to the windows of the keeper's quarters, suggesting light from within mixing with light from without. The detail took the painting from good to genuinely compelling.

"You've been studying the lighthouse's history," he said, shifting the subject away from his own creative avoidance. "Winnie mentioned you were asking questions."

"I found a journal in my cottage." Her brush strokes remained steady, but he heard caution enter her voice. "Old lighthouse keeper records. Some of the entries reference things that don't quite match the official history."

"Like what?"

"Just things…" She stared at her canvas, avoiding him. "Your town's lighthouse has quite a history."

Grant processed this carefully. He'd grown up hearing vague stories about the lighthouse's past, stories that always seemed to end just before the interesting parts. Nothing documented. The kind of local legend that added color to the town's history without requiring proof.

"What does Winnie say about it?"

"She confirms her ancestors kept the journal. Says there's truth in it, but some things need to stay buried. She also said some people would prefer the whole history stayed buried, including the developers trying to buy the property."

That caught Grant's full attention. Oceanside Development had been circling the lighthouse property for over a year, making increasingly aggressive purchase offers. Winnie had rebuffed them repeatedly, but they kept pushing. The company specialized in converting historic properties into luxury resort accommodations. They'd gutted three buildings in nearby towns already, destroying local character in pursuit of tourist revenue. They also had their eye on waterfront property in town.

"If there's legitimate historical significance beyond the lighthouse's normal function," he said slowly, "that could strengthen Winnie's position against development. Historic preservation protections go deeper if you can document multiple layers of use."

"That's what I thought."

Her interest in the lighthouse surprised him. She was just someone passing through on her way to somewhere else. Getting involved with researching the lighthouse's history meant acknowledging that she might stay and that she might become part of the community he'd been trying to protect from exactly this kind of outsider.

Except she wasn't treating the lighthouse like a curiosity. She was treating it like a home that deserved protection.

"I'm actually learning a lot about the lighthouse and Starlight Shores." Her lips rose in a brief smile.

"But no one just shares information. They share information, food, and family stories."

"Is that a problem?"

"I don't know yet." Her honesty was becoming familiar. "I came here wanting to be left alone. Everyone keeps being nice to me anyway."

He surprised himself by laughing. "Yeah, we're terrible that way. Winnie's trained the whole town to adopt strays whether they want adopting or not."

"Is that what you are? A stray?"

The question hit closer than she probably intended. "More like a boomerang. Left and came back."

"But you stayed. Built something here. That's different from just returning."

He looked out at the waves slowly rolling to shore. "Is it? Sometimes I wonder if I'm building something or just hiding from something."

He turned back to her. She added a final highlight to the keeper's quarters windows, and the painting suddenly felt complete. The light balanced perfectly with the shadow, the solid structure grounded by the atmospheric sky. It was beautiful and sad. Maybe hopeful too.

"I don't think those are opposites," she said finally. "Maybe you can hide and still build something. I don't know. Eventually, maybe the building matters more than the hiding."

The observation felt uncomfortably accurate.

He'd spent all these years telling himself he was creating something meaningful with the gallery, supporting local artists, and preserving the town's culture. All true. But also true was that he'd used those good works to avoid risking his own art again and his own vulnerability.

He changed the subject. "Your painting. It's finished, isn't it?"

She studied her work. "I think so. I might adjust the shadow balance once it dries, but the core feels right."

"You should show it at the Springtide Festival at the gallery."

Her shoulders tensed immediately. "No."

"Emily—"

"I'm not ready for that." Her voice carried an edge of panic that hadn't been there moments before. "This is just practice. Getting my hand back. It's not gallery work."

"That's not what I see."

"Then you're seeing wrong." She began cleaning her brushes with sharp, defensive movements. "I appreciate you looking. But I'm painting for myself right now. Not for exhibition."

He heard the fear underneath her refusal. He knew that paralysis. That certainty that showing work meant exposing yourself to judgment you couldn't survive. The difference was he'd let that fear win for seven years. Emily was at least creating again, even if she couldn't yet share it.

He nodded. "Okay, but when you're ready, the offer stands."

Her hands slowed on her cleaning rag. She looked at him with surprise, maybe having expected an argument. "Thank you."

"For what?"

"For not pushing. People always want to push past where you're ready to go."

He nodded again. "Yeah. Doesn't help, though. Just makes the wall higher."

They stood in companionable silence while Emily finished putting her supplies away. The wind had picked up slightly, and the temperature was climbing toward the day's full heat. He should head to the gallery. He had a lot of work to do. Instead, he heard himself say, "I was going to grab coffee at Harbor Brew. Want to join me? Once you're done here?"

Emily paused with her hand on the easel, and surprise flickered across her face. "I look like I've been painting in the wind for three hours."

"So? It's Starlight Shores. Nobody dresses up for coffee."

She laughed, and the genuine sound transformed her wary expression. "Fair point. Let me get this back to my cottage. I could be there in twenty minutes?"

"I'll meet you there."

He walked away before she could change her mind, before he could change his own mind. His phone buzzed with a message from the gallery assistant about a delivery question, grounding him back in practical concerns. He should be asking himself what he was doing, inviting Emily further into his life when he'd spent weeks trying to keep her at arm's length.

But the truth was simpler than his complicated justifications. He wanted to have coffee with someone who understood trying to create again after failure. Someone who saw the difference between hiding and healing because she was walking that same uncertain line.

Maybe that made him selfish, looking for understanding instead of offering it. Or maybe it made him human and finally willing to admit he wasn't as okay as he pretended to be.

CHAPTER 16

Emily arrived at Harbor Brew with paint still under her fingernails. She'd scrubbed them twice, but the ultramarine blue had already set. At least her hair looked decent after she'd twisted it into a French braid.

Grant had claimed a corner table away from the morning rush. He stood when she approached, a gesture that caught her off guard. When was the last time someone had stood for her? Daniel never had.

"Thanks for coming." He pulled out her chair.

"Thanks for asking." She settled into the seat while he signaled the server.

The coffee shop was busy with the morning crowd. Locals chatted at nearby tables, their conversations mixing with the espresso machine's hiss. Photos of the town taken over the years covered the walls, and a community bulletin board overflowed with colorful flyers. The whole place felt lived-in and welcoming.

Jan came over and smiled at Emily. "Welcome back. Hope you're adjusting to life in Starlight Shores."

"I am. Thank you."

"What can I get you?"

"Just a cappuccino. Thanks."

"And I'll have coffee. Black," Grant added.

"Be back in a flash."

For a moment, they sat in awkward silence. She traced a pattern in the grain of the wooden table, wondering why she'd agreed to this. She'd come to Starlight Shores to be alone, not to have coffee with attractive gallery owners who made her nervous.

Jan brought their coffee, breaking the awkward silence. She wrapped her hands around the warm cup and inhaled the rich aroma. Grant did the same, and she noticed his fingers were stained too. Not with paint, but with the kind of ink that came from handling newspapers and documents.

"You've been researching," she observed.

He glanced at his hands and grimaced. "Old habit. I still read multiple newspapers every morning. Can't seem to switch to digital."

"Physical newspapers?"

"Three of them. Local, regional, and the Times. My ex used to complain about the mess."

The mention of his ex created an opening. Emily wasn't sure she wanted to take it, but curiosity won. "How long were you married?"

"Never made it that far. We were together four years, engaged for the last one." His jaw tightened. "She was a curator. Miranda Keller. Maybe you knew her?"

She searched her memory. "The name sounds familiar. Tall brunette? Very polished?"

"That's her." His laugh held no humor. "We met at a gallery opening in Brooklyn. She seemed to get what I was trying to do with my art. Encouraged me to push boundaries and take risks."

He paused to sip his coffee. She waited, recognizing the look of someone deciding how much truth to share.

"We opened a gallery together," he continued. "Put everything I had into it. Money, time, and creative energy. I thought we were building something meaningful, supporting emerging artists, and creating a space for experimental work."

"What happened?"

"She happened." The bitterness crept into his voice. "I discovered she'd been negotiating to sell our gallery to a Manhattan dealer. Had been for months. Positioning herself for a big curator position while planning to leave me behind."

"She betrayed you."

"Completely. But the worst part?" He met her

eyes. "She told me my work was too regional. Too limited for the New York market. That I was holding her back from real success."

She winced. How many times had she heard similar dismissals? Your work is derivative. You're riding on Franklin's reputation. You don't have your own voice.

"I'm so sorry," she said quietly.

"Yeah, well." He shrugged, but tension remained in his shoulders. "I came home after that. Opened this gallery to do things differently. Support local artists without the politics and exploitation."

"But you stopped creating your own work."

His hands stilled on his cup. "I have."

"I recognize the look. The way you watch me paint. Like you're hungry for something you won't let yourself have."

Silence stretched between them. She worried she'd overstepped, but Grant finally nodded.

"Seven years," he admitted. "Haven't touched my tools in seven years."

"Why?"

"Because what if she was right? What if my work really is limited and regional and not worth anything beyond this small town?"

The raw honesty in his question made her pause. She knew that fear intimately. It lived in her bones and whispered in her ear every time she picked up a brush. "Can I tell you something?"

He nodded.

"When Franklin was dying, his son Julian accused me of manipulating him. Said I was stealing his father's legacy and passing off my work as Franklin's. My husband believed him. Daniel left me in the middle of the scandal because he didn't want it to affect his academic career."

"I'm sorry, Emily."

"The investigation cleared me. I had documentation, contracts, and Franklin's own written wishes. But it didn't matter. The art world had already decided I was guilty." She managed a bitter smile. "Apparently, it made a better story than the truth."

"What was the truth?"

She traced the rim of her cup. "Franklin asked me to help finish his final series. We worked together until he couldn't hold a brush anymore. Completing those paintings was the hardest thing I'd ever done because every stroke reminded me I was losing him."

Her voice cracked on the last words. He reached across the table, not quite touching her hand but close enough that she felt the warmth.

"That's why you stopped painting?" he asked.

"Every time I picked up a brush, I heard Julian's voice calling me a fraud. Heard Daniel saying my reputation was toxic." She met Grant's eyes. "So I ran. Came here thinking I could hide from all of it."

"Is it working?"

"No." The admission surprised her with its simplicity. "Because you can't hide from yourself. And I'm still an artist, even when I'm terrified to create."

Grant turned his cup in slow circles. "Miranda told me supporting other artists was noble but ultimately empty if I wasn't creating myself. I told myself she was wrong. That running the gallery was enough."

"Is it?"

"No." He echoed her honesty. "It's necessary and meaningful, but it's not enough. I miss making things. Miss the physical work of creating. Miss discovering what I'm trying to say through the process of creating."

She understood completely. Teaching art had been rewarding, but it couldn't replace the essential need to create. That drive lived deeper than career or reputation.

"You know what the worst part is?" He continued. "I've turned the gallery into my identity. The noble defender of local art against commercial corruption. But really, I'm just scared."

"Of what?"

"Of trying again, failing, and proving Miranda right. Or discovering I really don't have anything important to say."

She reached over and covered his hand. "But

what if she was wrong? What if your work matters precisely because it's rooted in this place and these people?"

He studied her face. "You don't think commercial success corrupts artistic vision?"

"I think that's a false choice. Franklin was commercially successful and still created profound work. The problem isn't success. It's when success becomes the only measure of value."

"I've been pretty rigid about it, haven't I?"

"We all build walls where we've been hurt. I've built plenty of my own." She pulled her hand back and wrapped it around her coffee.

They sat quietly while the coffee shop bustled around them. She felt something shifting between them. Not attraction exactly, though that hummed beneath the surface. More like recognition.

"Would you like to see something?" Grant asked suddenly.

"What?"

"My dad's studio. Where I used to work before..." He gestured vaguely. "Before everything."

She understood the enormity of this invitation. Studios were sacred spaces, especially abandoned ones.

"Are you sure?"

"No." His honesty made her smile. "But I'd like to show you anyway. If you're interested."

She was interested. More than she should be.

But sitting here with Grant, sharing their parallel wounds, she felt less alone than she had in years.

"I'd like that."

His smile transformed his face. For a moment, she glimpsed the artist he'd been before disappointment hardened him.

"Fair warning," he said as they stood. "I haven't been there in months. It might be a mess."

"I don't mind a mess. And thank you for telling me. You know, about Miranda and the gallery and everything."

"Thank you for listening. And for sharing your story too." He placed his hand gently on her back and led her to the door.

CHAPTER 17

Grant's family home sat three blocks from the harbor on a quiet street lined with live oaks. The two-story Victorian had weathered blue paint and white trim that needed touching up. A wraparound porch held mismatched furniture and wind chimes that played soft melodies in the breeze.

"Mom keeps threatening to repaint, but she can't decide on colors."

Emily understood the hesitation. Some houses held too many memories to change easily.

The front door opened before they reached it. A woman with silver hair and Grant's blue eyes smiled warmly.

"You must be Emily. I'm Margaret. Grant mentioned he was bringing company." She stepped aside to let them in.

"Thank you for having me." She felt suddenly uncertain.

"Any friend of Grant's is welcome here. Besides, I've heard about your paintings. It's always nice to meet another artist."

The house smelled like flowers from the numerous vases scattered around the room and something baking in the kitchen. Family photos covered the walls. She glimpsed Grant at various ages, always with paint or tools in his hands.

"The studio's out back. Through here." Grant seemed nervous now.

They walked through a kitchen with herbs growing on the windowsill. The back door led to a covered walkway connecting the house to a converted garage. Grant paused with his hand on the studio door.

"I should warn you. Nothing's been moved since Dad died. Mom won't let me change anything."

"Grant, that's not true. I just think someone should use it before we pack it away." Margaret's voice held a hint of reproach.

He opened the door.

The smell hit Emily first. Paint, turpentine, and dust. She smiled with recognition. Every artist's studio carried that particular mixture. It meant home in ways nothing else could.

Afternoon light flooded through the windows. Canvases lined the walls. An easel stood in the center with brushes still arranged on the side table as if the artist had just stepped out.

"Oh." The word escaped before she could stop it.

The paintings drew her forward. Coastal landscapes filled most of the frames. Not the pretty postcards tourists expected, but the real Gulf. Moody skies threatening storms. Shrimp boats working before dawn. The lighthouse standing patiently through changing weather.

She stopped before a painting of the harbor at sunset. The light captured that specific moment when day surrendered to dusk. Gold melted into purple while working boats headed home.

"This is exceptional. The way he built up the waves. See how the transparency here creates depth?" She studied the brushwork.

Grant moved beside her. "He never thought they were good enough for galleries. Said people wanted prettier versions of the coast."

"He was painting truth instead of fantasy. That's always a harder sell. But look at this technique. He understood light like the Impressionists did. Not copying, but translating."

She moved to another painting. This one showed the aftermath of a hurricane. Debris was scattered across the sand while survivors picked through the wreckage. Beautiful and heartbreaking at once.

"When was this?"

"Hurricane Donna in the 1960s." Margaret joined them. "Jack spent weeks documenting the recovery. Sold most of the paintings to tourists for grocery money."

Her heart ached at the waste. These paintings belonged in museums. Instead, they probably hung in random living rooms, picked up as souvenirs by people who didn't understand their value.

"May I?" She gestured toward a stack of unframed canvases.

Margaret nodded. "Please. It's nice to see someone appreciate them properly."

She carefully sorted through the paintings. Each one revealed more of Thomas Stone's gift. He'd captured the working waterfront with respect and authenticity. No romanticizing. No false nostalgia. Just honest observation rendered with remarkable skill.

She turned to Grant. "Your father understood this place. Really understood it. Not the surface pretty, but the actual life here."

"Regional artist. That's what gallery owners called him when he tried to show outside Florida." Grant's voice carried old bitterness.

"Their loss. Though I understand the frustration. The art world loves categories. Regional. Outsider. Folk. Anything to avoid admitting they might have missed something important."

"Show her yours." Margaret nudged Grant. "Don't look at me like that. She's an artist. She'll understand."

He hesitated. Emily understood. Showing old work felt like exposing past selves you'd outgrown.

"Only if you want to." She gave him an out.

He crossed to a corner where several sculptures sat on shelves. The first piece made her lean closer. He'd combined driftwood with rusted metal and fragments of blue glass.

He lifted the sculpture. "This is from my New York period. Before I figured out nobody wanted contemplation about urban decay from someone who said y'all."

She took the piece carefully. The weight surprised her. He'd hidden steel framework inside the wood, creating a structure that wasn't immediately visible. The glass caught the light and threw blue shadows.

"This is sophisticated work. The way you've balanced found objects with intentional intervention. I can see why galleries noticed you."

"For about five minutes."

"Commercial attention and artistic merit aren't the same thing. You know that."

He showed her more pieces. Each one revealed careful thought and skilled execution. He'd explored how objects transformed through weather and time. How human intentions yielded to natural forces.

"You were asking real questions with these." Emily studied a piece incorporating fishing net and copper wire. "About preservation and change. About what survives and why."

"Miranda said they were too crafted. That I was trying to control materials that should stay raw."

"Miranda was protecting her territory. Classic curator move. Make you doubt yourself so you need her approval."

His eyes widened, and he nodded. "That's exactly what she did."

"I've seen it before. Franklin protected me from most of it. But after he died, I learned fast how the game worked."

Margaret had been quiet, but now she spoke. "You both carry such wounds. Makes me grateful Jack never had to navigate that world."

Emily heard the pain beneath her words. A different kind of wound. Watching someone you love create beauty that the world wouldn't fairly value.

"Your husband's work will last long after trendy gallery shows are forgotten. This is the real thing."

"Thank you." Margaret's voice softened. "Would you like to stay for dinner? Nothing fancy, but I made pot roast."

She glanced at Grant. He looked vulnerable standing among his father's paintings and his own abandoned sculptures. She understood. Sometimes the past felt too heavy to carry alone.

"I'd like that, if it's not too much trouble."

"Wonderful." Margaret headed for the door. "Grant, show her the rest. I'll call when it's ready."

They stood alone in the studio. The dust they'd disturbed floated through the afternoon sun.

"Thank you for showing me both your father's work and yours."

He ran his finger along one of his sculptures. "I haven't been in here in years. Kept telling myself I was too busy."

"I know that lie. Told it to myself too."

"What changed?"

"I got tired of letting fear win. Tired of letting other people's opinions matter more than my need to create."

He studied her face. "Is it easier now?"

"No. But necessary. Some days I feel like myself again. Other days, I'm sure everyone was right about me."

"They weren't."

"You don't know that."

"I've seen your work. That's enough."

The certainty in his voice made her pause before she spoke. "We... We should help your mother." She turned toward the door before he could see her face.

"Emily?" He caught her arm. "I'm glad you're here. Not just in Starlight Shores. Here, seeing this."

"Me too." The words felt inadequate but true.

They headed into the house. Margaret had set the dining table with everyday dishes and mason jar glasses that somehow felt more welcoming than fine china ever could. They joined her at the table.

"Grant tells me you're helping Winnie with some historical research." Margaret passed the green beans.

"Just trying to piece together some lighthouse history. Though I'm not sure I'm qualified." Emily took a small serving.

"Nonsense. Fresh eyes see things we locals miss." Margaret's smile held genuine warmth.

Grant poured sweet tea from a pitcher beaded with condensation. "Mom's being modest. She knows more town history than anyone except Winnie."

Margaret's eyes sparkled. "Well, when you marry into a family like the Stones, you learn to pay attention. Tom's great-grandfather helped build half the houses in the historic district."

Emily sensed the pride beneath those words. Not the showy kind, but the quiet satisfaction of belonging somewhere.

"Tell her about Dad and the lighthouse painting." Grant settled back in his chair.

Margaret laughed. "Oh, that story. Jack spent three months painting the lighthouse during different weather conditions. Got up at all hours, drove me crazy with his alarm going off at four in the morning."

"Why so early?"

"He wanted to capture it during storms. Said that's when the lighthouse showed its true purpose. Not the pretty postcard version, but the working beacon that actually saved lives."

"The Coast Guard commissioned the painting eventually," Grant added. "Hangs in their station now."

"After we nearly lost the house paying bills." Margaret's tone stayed light, but Emily heard the steel underneath. "That's what I tried to tell Grant when he was young. Art's not about choosing between integrity and survival. It's about finding ways to do both."

The words hit home. She had been so focused on either-or. Either artistic purity or selling out. Either Franklin's protégé or her own artist. Maybe those were false choices too.

"More pot roast?" Margaret offered.

"Yes, please." She held out her plate. The conversation drifted to safer topics of town events, garden challenges, and the new bakery opening next month. She found herself relaxing into the rhythm of a family dinner. No agenda. No performance required. Just food and stories and the kind of easy warmth she'd forgotten existed.

Grant guided Emily along the sandy path that wound between the dunes. The moon cast everything in silver, making the familiar route look almost magical. He'd walked this way hundreds of times, but tonight felt different.

Emily stumbled on a piece of driftwood hidden in the shadows. He caught her arm and steadied her before she could fall.

"Thanks." She looked up at him, her face illuminated by moonlight.

"These paths can be tricky at night." He kept his hand on her arm a moment longer than necessary. Then, without really thinking about it, he took her hand. "Better this way."

Her fingers intertwined with his, warm and slightly rough from paint and turpentine. They walked in comfortable silence while the lighthouse beam swept over them in steady intervals. The night air carried salt and the rhythmic sound of the waves.

At her cottage door, Emily turned to face him. "Thank you for today. I had a really nice time."

"Me too." He squeezed her hand gently before letting go. "And think about showing your work at the Springtide Festival. You're really talented. People should see your work."

She laughed. "I could say the same to you."

"Touché."

She smiled, that genuine smile he was starting to recognize. "Good night, Grant."

"Good night." He waited until she was safely inside before heading home. The lighthouse beam circled overhead, cutting through the darkness.

He shoved his hands in his pockets and walked slowly, not ready for the evening to end. What a day. He'd actually shown someone his sculptures. Not just someone. Emily. And she'd understood them. Understood him, maybe. The way she'd looked at his father's paintings and recognized their worth beyond tourist appeal. The way she'd traced the lines of his driftwood pieces without judgment.

He thought about her hands covered in paint and the fierce concentration on her face when she worked. The courage it took to pick up that brush after two years of silence. Maybe that was the thing. Maybe courage was contagious. Emily was painting again despite everything that had happened to her, creating new work even though the world had torn her last pieces apart.

Grant paused at his gallery door and looked

back toward the lighthouse. The beam swept past again, steady and sure. Maybe he could try again too. Not for anyone else. Not to prove Miranda wrong or vindicate his father's legacy. Just to create. To see what was still inside him waiting to take shape.

CHAPTER 18

Winnie set the teapot on the kitchen table as Sally came through the back door, bakery box in hand. Tuesday afternoon. Same as last week, same as the week before that, same as however many years they'd been doing this. Sally dropped into her chair by the window, the one with the faded cushion she'd brought over herself a decade ago because Winnie's chairs were "hard as church pews."

"Lemon cream puffs." Sally opened the box and pushed it across the table. "The new girl at the bakery made them. Thought we'd see if she knows what she's doing."

Winnie poured tea into two cups—hers with the chipped handle that she kept meaning to replace, Sally's with the roses that had been red once and were now just a suggestion of pink. "After those chocolate things you brought last month, I'm not getting my hopes up."

"Those were perfectly fine chocolate things."

"They tasted like cardboard dipped in cocoa powder."

Sally laughed and took a cream puff, biting into it. Powdered sugar scattered across her navy shirt. She didn't bother brushing it off. "These are better. Try one."

Winnie did. The lemon hit first, tart and bright, then the cream underneath. Not too sweet. "All right. The new girl can stay."

"High praise from you." Sally took another bite, catching a bit of cream that escaped with her thumb. "I'll let her know she passed the Winnie Lockhart test."

"Don't you dare."

They ate in comfortable silence for a few minutes. The afternoon light came through the window at a low angle, catching a streak of dust on the far edge of the table. Winnie got up, grabbed a dish towel, and swiped at the dust. Hardly anyone ever sat in that seat. It had been her father's. She settled back in her chair and took a sip of tea. She could hear the faint crash of waves from the beach, muffled by distance and the cottage walls.

Winnie mindlessly folded the towel. "Have you finalized the vendor list for Springtide yet?"

"Mostly. I've got confirmations from about thirty

people. Still waiting to hear back from that jewelry maker in Clearwater. The one who does the sea glass pieces."

"Oh, I remember her. The necklace with the green glass?"

"That's her. She said she'd let me know by the end of the week, but that was last week, so." Sally shrugged. "I'll call her again tomorrow."

"Her work is beautiful."

"It is. Which is why I want her there." Sally picked up her tea and held it without drinking, letting the warmth seep into her hands. "Of course, the mayor wants to expand the vendor area again."

"Again?"

"She thinks we should take over the whole parking lot behind the community center. Set up twice as many booths."

"Where would people park?"

"Exactly what I said. She told me we could arrange a shuttle from the church lot." Sally rolled her eyes. "A shuttle. For Springtide. Like we're running some kind of major operation."

"She does like her big ideas."

"She likes the idea of big ideas. The actual logistics, she leaves to everyone else." Sally shook her head. "I told her we'd discuss it at the next planning meeting. Which means I have a week to figure out how to talk her out of it without making her dig in."

Winnie smiled. Sally had been managing difficult people on the festival committee for fifteen years. She'd figure it out. She always did.

Sally set her cup down with a small clink against the saucer. "I saw Grant and Emily in town the other day."

"Did you?"

"They looked comfortable together."

"Did they?"

Sally gave her a look. "Winnie. I've heard from at least four people this week about the two of them. You're going to pretend you don't know anything?"

Winnie added a spoonful of honey to her tea and stirred it slowly, watching the honey dissolve in amber spirals. "I know Grant asked her to show her work at the festival."

"And?"

"She said no." Winnie sighed. "He's asked twice. She keeps finding reasons to refuse."

Sally frowned, reaching for another cream puff. "That's a shame. I know you said the painting she did of your grandfather's study was wonderful. Full of emotion."

"Emily's talented. More talented than she knows or admits." Winnie set her cup down. "But that awful situation in Chicago did a number on her confidence."

"That Julian fellow, right? Franklin's son?"

"Yes." Winnie's jaw tightened. "And he's still at

it, apparently. Emily mentioned he sent her another message last week."

"That's horrible." Sally shook her head, genuine anger flashing across her face. "Emily's been cleared of any wrongdoing. The courts said so. What more does this Julian person want?"

"I don't think it's about the truth for him. It's about blame. About grief, maybe." Winnie picked up her tea again. "But whatever his reasons, it's working. Emily's terrified to put her work out there."

They sat with that for a moment. The clock on the wall ticked. Somewhere outside, a car door slammed.

Sally leaned back in her chair, studying Winnie's face. "Grant must really believe in her if he keeps asking."

"He does." Winnie couldn't help the small smile that tugged at her lips, and Sally caught it immediately.

"What was that?"

"What was what?"

"That. That little—" Sally gestured vaguely at Winnie's face. "You know something."

"I don't know anything." She tried for innocence, focusing intently on her tea.

Sally laughed. "Winnie Lockhart, I've known you your whole life. Don't even try."

Winnie sighed. There was no point trying to

hide things from Sally. Never had been, not since they were seven years old and Sally had figured out that Winnie was the one who'd accidentally broken the window in the Wilsons' shed. "Fine. I think there might be something between them. Or starting to be."

"Really?" Sally's eyes lit up with genuine delight. "Tell me everything."

"There's not much to tell yet. But he walked her home from dinner at his mother's house last week. And I've seen him at the beach in the mornings when she paints. He says he's just walking, but that man hasn't taken morning beach walks since high school."

"Margaret must be pleased."

"I haven't talked to her about it. But yes, I imagine she's noticed." Winnie traced the rim of her cup with one finger. "They're good for each other, I think. They understand what the other's been through."

"Both got hurt by people they trusted." Sally nodded slowly. "That's not a small thing."

"No, it's not." Winnie stared out the window again, watching clouds drift past the lighthouse. "Grant's been closed off since he returned to Starlight Shores. Hasn't let anyone close. But with Emily..." She trailed off, searching for the right words. "I don't know…"

"Maybe they're both ready now. Sometimes

timing matters more than we want to admit."

"Maybe." Winnie hoped so. Both of them deserved something good after the past few years.

Sally reached for the last cream puff, then stopped. "You want this?"

"Go ahead."

Sally took it and bit in. More powdered sugar fell. "What about Melissa? She settling in all right?"

"She is, actually. She and Emily have become friends."

"Have they?"

"I saw them on the beach the other morning. Melissa had her camera, and Emily had her sketchbook. They weren't talking much, just walking together." Winnie remembered how they'd looked, two figures moving along the waterline in the early light. Comfortable in the silence. "I think it's good for both of them."

"Melissa seems like she keeps to herself."

"She does. But she's coming out of it a little. The lighthouse is good for her, I think. Quiet. Room to breathe."

Sally finished the cream puff and dusted off her hands. "I should get back. The store's been busy this week."

"That's good."

"Good for the bank account. Less good for my feet." Sally stood and carried her cup to the sink, rinsing it out of habit even though Winnie would wash it properly later. "I keep meaning to hire someone part-time."

"You should."

"I know. I just haven't found the time to actually do it."

"Make time."

Sally laughed, drying her hands on the towel by the sink. "You're one to talk. When's the last time you took a day off?"

Winnie didn't answer because Sally had a point and they both knew it.

Sally came back around the table and hugged her, a quick, tight squeeze. "Friday night? Save me a seat by the fire."

"Always do."

Winnie watched from the doorway as Sally walked across the courtyard toward the parking area, her friend's figure moving with the same brisk energy she'd had at seventeen. Some things never changed.

CHAPTER 19

Emily picked up the festival flyer Grant had left on her kitchen counter. The Springtide Festival was three days of art, music, and celebration. He'd asked her—multiple times—to display her work for the festival.

But that was three days of being visible. She set the flyer down as if it might bite her.

She'd managed to avoid crowds for weeks now. The farmers' market was bad enough with its handful of vendors and early morning shoppers. But this? This would be hundreds of people. Maybe thousands.

Stop being dramatic. It's a small-town festival, not a Chicago gallery opening.

The thought of Chicago made her feel physically ill. She pushed away memories of reporters shoving microphones in her face, gallery patrons whispering behind their hands, and Daniel's cold announcement that he needed to create distance from the situation.

Her phone buzzed. A text from Grant: *No pressure. Just think about it.*

Right. No pressure. Just display her work publicly for the first time since her world imploded. What could go wrong?

She grabbed her coffee and headed for the studio. She'd been painting every morning now, losing herself in the work the way she used to. The canvases lined the walls, filled with lighthouses at dawn, the keeper's quarters, and a seascape with a fiery sunset and a storm brewing in the distance.

They were good. She knew they were good. That terrified her more than if they'd been mediocre.

A knock interrupted her spiraling thoughts. She went to the door, and Winnie stood with a plate of something that smelled like cinnamon.

Winnie held out the plate. "Coffee cake. Made too much for the historical society meeting."

Emily stepped aside to let her in. Winnie had a way of showing up exactly when Emily's thoughts turned darkest.

"Grant mentioned the festival exhibition." Winnie settled at the kitchen table as if she belonged there.

"He did?" Emily cut two slices of coffee cake, buying time.

"It would mean a lot to him if you showed your work."

"I know. I'm just not sure I'm ready." The cake was perfect. It was moist and sweet with a crumbly top. Everything Winnie made was perfect.

"Ready for what, exactly?"

"Ready to be that person again. The artist. The one people look at and judge and—"

"The one who makes people stop and look twice?"

"That's not how it ended last time."

Winnie didn't look away. "No. But that's not how it has to end this time."

She took another bite of her coffee cake. "What if someone recognizes my name? What if they do an internet search and find all those articles? What if—"

"What if they see your work and feel something true?"

She thought of the paintings in her studio. Each one had come from a real place, an honest place. Not the calculated compositions she'd created in Chicago, always wondering what the critics would say. These were different.

"The festival celebrates our town's heritage. Your paintings capture something essential about this place. About what it means to keep the light burning."

"You're very good at this."

"At what?"

"Making me feel guilty."

Winnie laughed. "I'm not trying to make you feel guilty. I'm trying to help you see that hiding isn't actually keeping you safe. It's keeping you stuck."

Emily walked to the window. The lighthouse stood tall against the morning sky, its white tower catching the light. She'd painted it from every angle, in every weather. She knew the building now. Every crack, every curve, how the light made it change.

"Grant's taking a risk too. Asking you. He doesn't invite just anyone to exhibit."

"I know." She'd seen his gallery and understood what he was trying to build. A space for authentic work, for artists who captured truth rather than trends. The opposite of everything that had hurt them both.

"One painting. That's all he's asking. One painting to test the waters." Winnie stood, brushing crumbs from her hands.

After Winnie left, Emily returned to her studio. The paintings watched her from the walls. Which one could she bear to let strangers see? The dawn lighthouse, all uncertainty and hope? The keeper's quarters, heavy with secrets?

Her phone buzzed again. Melissa this time:

Heard about the festival. You should do it. We could be terrified together.

She smiled despite herself. Melissa was contributing photographs. It was her first public display since whatever had driven her to hide behind her camera. If Melissa could face her fears...

But Melissa's name isn't splashed across the internet with the word fraud attached to it.

She picked up her brush, not to paint but just to hold it. The weight felt right in her hand. Natural. Like it belonged there.

What if Winnie was right? What if hiding wasn't protecting her but imprisoning her?

Her paintings weren't just pretty pictures. They were investigations. Documentations. Honest work. The kind that made her nervous. The lighthouse had more stories than even Winnie knew, and Emily was uncovering them one brushstroke at a time.

Maybe that work deserved to be seen. Maybe the community that had sheltered her deserved to know what she'd discovered about their heritage. Maybe—

Maybe you're overthinking this.

Grant had asked for one painting. One. She could survive one painting in a small-town festival exhibition. She could smile politely at visitors, deflect personal questions, and keep the focus on the work itself. She'd become an expert at deflection these past months.

She pulled out her phone and stared at Grant's message. Her thumbs hovered over the keyboard. Such a simple response—yes or no—but it felt like signing something legally binding.

She typed before she could change her mind: "One painting. My choice which one. No artist bio."

His response came quickly: "Perfect. Thank you."

Three words, but she read relief in them. Maybe even hope. Grant was rebuilding too, in his own way. Maybe that was something.

Emily looked around her studio again. One painting. She could do this.

Couldn't she?

A few days later, Grant texted again: *Thinking more about your work. The lighthouse interior, especially. Would you consider showing three pieces instead of one?*

Three. The number made her stomach flip.

She walked into her studio. The lighthouse interior leaned against the wall. Winnie's tears had validated something Emily hadn't dared believe. That she could still move people with her work. That she hadn't lost that essential thing that made her an artist.

The seascape on her easel caught the morning

light from the studio window. She'd painted it during a storm, trying to capture how the Gulf looked angry and beautiful at the same time.

Her phone buzzed again: *I know it's a bigger ask. But your work deserves to be seen properly. One painting doesn't tell a story. Three will.*

A story. Is that what she'd been painting? She moved to another canvas. It was the cottage courtyard at sunset. She'd captured the residents during one of Winnie's gatherings. Not portraits exactly, but suggestions of people finding community. She'd painted hints of Melissa's defensive posture as she talked with Clint, Sally's animated hands as she told some town gossip, and Winnie presiding over it all with quiet authority.

Three paintings would definitely tell a story. The question was whether she wanted that story told.

Emily picked up her phone and typed: *Let me think about it.*

Then she deleted it.

She typed again: *Three feels like a lot.*

She tried two more times before finally sending her message: *Okay, three.*

And somehow, the one painting became three paintings. She couldn't resist his enthusiasm for her work.

CHAPTER 20

"Programs?" Emily heard her own voice crack.

Winnie stood on Starfish Cottage's front porch and held out a glossy booklet. "For the Springtide Festival. Grant makes beautiful booklets with artist biographies, photos of featured works, and a map of exhibition spaces. They're collectors' items. People keep them for years."

Collectors' items. Searchable, shareable, permanent records connecting Emily Shaw to Starlight Shores, Florida. Anyone looking for her would only need to search her name plus "art exhibition" to find her exact location.

Her heart did a double beat. Of course! She should have thought of this when she said yes to showing her work.

Julian could find her.

She'd been so focused on creating again, on

healing, and on this small community that had welcomed her, that she'd somehow convinced herself she could stay invisible. That painting in Starlight Shores was different from painting in Chicago. That a small-town festival wouldn't register on Julian's radar.

But of course it would. He had money, resources, and unlimited spite. He probably had search alerts set up on her name. The moment those festival programs went online—and they would, because every event posted their materials digitally now—he'd know exactly where to find her.

"Emily? Are you all right?" Winnie stepped inside. "You've gone white."

"I... How public are these programs?"

"Very. Grant posts them on the gallery website, the festival website, and social media. The tourism board shares them. Why?"

Because Julian would see them. Because he'd come here, to this place she'd started to think of as safe. He'd stand in front of her paintings and call her a fraud again, this time in front of everyone she'd begun to care about. He'd confront her in front of Grant, Winnie, Sally, Melissa, and the entire community that had slowly, carefully welcomed her.

She couldn't let that happen. She couldn't drag them into her scandal.

"I need to withdraw from the festival." The

words tumbled out. "I'm sorry, Winnie, but I can't—I can't do this."

"Because of Julian Holloway." It wasn't a question. Winnie's voice held the calm certainty of someone who'd lived long enough to recognize fear when she saw it.

"Then you know why I can't put my name in a public festival program. He'll find me. He'll come here and destroy everything, and I won't—I can't—put Grant's gallery at risk. Or your lighthouse. Or—"

"Or face him again. That's what you're really afraid of." Winnie's tone was gentle but unflinching.

"Of course I'm afraid!" Her voice rose. "You didn't see what he did in Chicago. The reporters, the accusations, the way everyone I trusted just... disappeared. My husband left me. My gallery dropped me. My teaching position ended. Even after being cleared, I couldn't get any of it back because Julian had poisoned everything."

"So your plan is to let him keep poisoning your life from a distance?"

She opened her mouth to argue, then closed it.

"You came here to hide. Fine. Everyone needs that sometimes. But you've been catching your breath for a while now. At some point, you have to actually breathe out, rebuild your strength, and then stand up again."

"I'm not strong enough."

"Those paintings say otherwise. Those paintings say you're exactly strong enough. You created something true despite everything Julian Holloway tried to take from you. Your voice is right there on that canvas. Everything he tried to take is still yours."

The cottage suddenly felt too small, and the walls pressed in. "What if I show my work and he comes here, and it happens again? What if he convinces everyone that I'm a fraud? What if—"

"What if you spend the rest of your life running?" Winnie moved to the doorway of the studio. "This is extraordinary work, Emily. It deserves to be seen. You deserve to be seen. And yes, Julian might find out. He might come here. But you know what? He'll find a community that actually knows you this time. People who've watched you heal, seen you create, and witnessed your character firsthand."

"Winnie, please—"

"Grant. This is about Grant too, isn't it? You're not just afraid of Julian destroying your reputation again. You're afraid of what Julian might do to someone you're starting to care about."

Her face heated. Was she that obvious?

"That young man has his own scars. That ex-girlfriend of his did her own damage when she betrayed him. He opened that gallery knowing it might fail. Supports artists who might never sell.

That man chooses risk every single day." She tapped her phone screen. "Now it's your turn to choose."

"I need time to think—"

"You've had months to think. Thinking time is over." Winnie's voice held steel beneath the kindness. "Sometimes we need to be pushed off the cliff to remember we can fly."

"Or to confirm we'll crash." She heard the bitterness in her voice.

"Then you crash. And you get back up. That's what living looks like, Emily. Not hiding in a lighthouse cottage pretending you can make yourself small enough to disappear."

She walked into the studio and sank onto the stool beside her easel. Her hands found the familiar grooves worn into the wood from hours of sitting in this exact spot. Creating again had felt like coming home. But showing that creation to the world? That was different. That was a vulnerability she wasn't sure she could survive.

Her phone chimed. She pulled it from her pocket with trembling hands.

An email notification.

From an address she didn't recognize, but the subject line made her blood run cold: *Found you.*

She opened the email with fingers that had gone numb.

Emily,

Saw the festival listing. Already emailed the organizers about your history.

See you soon.

Julian

The phone slipped from her hand and clattered to the floor. Winnie was beside her immediately, retrieving the phone, reading the message.

"That…" Winnie's language turned surprisingly colorful for a lighthouse keeper. She grabbed her own phone. "I'm texting Grant. This changes things." Winnie sent the text without asking permission.

"It doesn't change anything. He's found me. He's already contacted the festival. It's over."

"Over? Emily Shaw, you listen to me." Winnie gripped Emily's shoulders, forcing eye contact. "That boy is a bully. And bullies only win when good people run away scared. Is that who you want to be? Someone who creates beautiful, honest work and then lets a damaged, grieving man destroy it because he can't face his own pain?"

"He'll ruin everything—"

"He'll try. But he won't succeed. Not this time." Winnie's certainty was unshakeable. "This time, you have a community. And most importantly, this time you're not going to run."

She wanted to argue. Wanted to say that Winnie didn't understand, that it was different, that Julian had resources and ruthlessness and nothing to lose. But a knock at the door interrupted her spiral.

Grant's voice carried through the door. "Winnie? Emily? It's me."

Winnie moved to let him in before Emily could protest. He came into the cottage and stepped into the studio, his expression concerned, and his eyes immediately found Emily's face. Whatever he saw there made him cross the room in three long strides.

"I was already on my way over when I got your text. What happened?"

"Show him the email," Winnie instructed.

Emily didn't want to. Didn't want to see Grant's expression change from concern to pity, or worse, from support to self-preservation. She picked up her phone and handed it to him without looking at his face.

The silence stretched. Finally, Grant spoke, his voice carefully controlled. "When did this come?"

"Minutes ago. Don't you see? I have to pull out of the festival now. He's already contacted the festival organizers, Grant. He'll poison everything before it even begins. I won't let him destroy your gallery's reputation—"

"My gallery's reputation?" His laugh held no humor. He moved to look at her painting on the easel, studying it with the intensity she'd come to recognize. "Emily, look at this. Really look at it."

"I know what it is—"

"Do you?" He turned back to her. "Because I see an artist who's found her voice again. I see work that's technically brilliant and emotionally honest. I see something that would be an honor to display in my gallery, scandal or no scandal."

"Julian will threaten lawsuits—"

"Let him threaten. We'll be ready if Julian shows up."

"You can't want this fight."

"I've been running from fights for seven years." Something hard entered Grant's expression. "Seven years of telling myself that supporting other artists was enough. That I didn't need to create or take risks or put myself out there again because Miranda taught me how painful that could be. But you know what I figured out watching you paint?"

She shook her head, not trusting her voice.

"Running doesn't make you safer." He stepped closer. "Julian is going to come after you whether you're in the festival or not. That email proves it. He found you anyway. So the only real question is if you face him as an artist showing honest work with a community behind you, or do you face him as someone who's still running, still letting him control your choices?"

She hated that Grant was right. Julian had found her. The hiding was over. She could keep running—pack up tonight, find another small town, start over again—or she could stand her ground for the first time since this nightmare began.

"Don't let fear make this choice. Let your art make it."

He set her phone gently on the work table and moved toward the door. Winnie followed, pausing long enough to squeeze Emily's hand. "You're scared. It's okay to be scared. Paint scared. Show up anyway."

Then they were gone, and she was alone with her paintings and Julian's threatening email.

She looked at her painting. At the morning light streaming through the windows, the lived-in warmth, the truth she'd captured about home and healing. This wasn't derivative. This wasn't fraud. This was hers.

And Julian Holloway had already taken enough from her.

Emily picked up her phone. Her hands shook as she started to text. The message was short: *Include my paintings. I'm done running.*

She hit send before she could change her mind.

Then she sat in her studio, watching the afternoon light shift across her canvas and waited for her hands to stop shaking. They didn't. But she picked up a brush anyway.

CHAPTER 21

The storm had reshaped the shoreline overnight. Grant walked along the beach Monday morning, stepping over fallen palm fronds and debris washed up from deeper waters. The air still carried that electric scent that followed Gulf storms, full of a mixture of salt, ozone, and plant matter.

He hadn't planned this detour. He usually took his morning walk, then headed to the gallery with coffee in hand, planning the day's tasks. But Emily's decision to exhibit her paintings had left him restless and unsettled.

The beach was deserted this early. Most locals knew to give the shore a day to settle after a storm. The waves still churned with unusual force, tossing new offerings onto the sand with each surge. They pushed ashore shells, seaweed, and the occasional jellyfish that he carefully sidestepped.

He spotted it half-buried near the water's edge. Something about its shape caught his eye. A piece of driftwood, twisted and bleached by salt and sun. Not particularly large—maybe three feet long—but its curves spoke of years battling currents.

Grant stopped and knelt beside it. The sand was cool and damp beneath his knees.

The wood had once been part of a larger tree, but the ocean had shaped it into something else entirely, something both broken and beautiful. The grain swirled in patterns that reminded him of the lighthouse's spiral staircase.

He brushed away the sand, revealing more of the wood's complex texture. His fingers traced the curves, feeling for weaknesses, for potential, for the thing hiding inside that only he could see.

Seven years.

It had been years since he'd touched raw materials with creative intent. Years of running a gallery, supporting other artists, and telling himself that was enough. Years of lying to himself.

He lifted the driftwood. It was lighter than it looked, hollowed by time and tide, but still strong and resilient. The core remained intact despite everything the Gulf had thrown at it.

He placed it back on the sand and stood, wiping his hands on his jeans. This was ridiculous. He had a gallery to run, a festival to organize, and artists depending on him. He didn't have time for creative indulgences.

What would Emily say?

The thought ambushed him. Emily, who now painted every morning with gradually increasing confidence. Emily, who had agreed to exhibit three paintings despite Julian Holloway's shadow still hanging over her.

If she could face her fears, what was his excuse?

He picked up the driftwood again, tucked it under his arm, and continued down the beach, eyes scanning the shoreline with new purpose. He found a twisted piece of metal, possibly from a boat damaged in the storm. Then he picked up a length of copper wire, green with patina, and a chunk of sea glass, its edges smoothed by years of tumbling in the sea.

By the time he reached the steps leading up from the beach, his arms were full. The gallery could wait an hour, maybe two.

His father's workshop hadn't been used in years. It still smelled the same. He hadn't changed anything since his father died, though he'd told himself it was to preserve his father's legacy rather than admit he was preserving the possibility of his own return.

Grant set his beach findings on the workbench. The tools waited in neat rows along the pegboard.

Pliers, files, wire cutters, and the small drill his father had given him when he was fourteen all hung on the wall in their proper places. All untouched for too long.

He ran his fingers over the driftwood again. He could see what it might become. The shape was already suggested in the curves.

Miranda's voice whispered in his mind.

He pushed the thought away. This wasn't about her. This wasn't about galleries or critics or commercial appeal. This was about the storm and the wood. Seven years of silence demanding an answer.

His hands selected a file. The familiarity of it settled something inside him. He began removing the splintered edges, working with rather than against the wood's natural grain. His body remembered this rhythm and the way his breath synchronized with each stroke of the file.

Time slipped. The morning light shifted across the workshop floor. He barely noticed.

The copper wire came next. He twisted it through the natural openings in the wood, creating a structure that complemented rather than competed with the driftwood's flow. The metal piece needed modification. He worked it carefully with pliers until it fit against the wood as if they had always belonged together.

This wasn't like his New York work. This was

about listening and letting the materials guide his hands rather than forcing his vision upon them.

He stepped back, surprised to find his shirt damp with sweat. How long had he been working? The sculpture wasn't finished, but it had taken form. The driftwood curved like a question mark, copper wire wrapping its length like memories. The metal piece provided anchoring weight. The sea glass caught light at precisely the angle where the wood's natural curve created a hollow.

It wasn't perfect. It wasn't sophisticated or theoretical. But it was honest in a way his previous work had never been.

His phone rang in his pocket. He glanced at his watch and shook his head. Nearly eleven. He'd lost three hours to this unexpected detour.

He washed his hands at the workshop sink, watching dirt and tiny splinters swirl down the drain. His palms bore the beginnings of blisters. The muscles in his forearms ached pleasantly. He felt more alive than he had in years.

He almost closed the workshop door without looking back. Almost walked away, back to just being the gallery owner rather than the artist. But something made him turn.

The sculpture waited in a shaft of sunlight. Imperfect. Unfinished. But started.

Sometimes starting was the hardest part. Emily had taught him that. She'd shown up on that beach at dawn and faced the blank canvas. He could do the same.

Maybe he could be that brave too.

Before he could change his mind, he grabbed his handiwork, his creation, his art, and headed back to the gallery.

CHAPTER 22

Emily stepped back from where Grant had just hung her lighthouse painting. The natural light caught the brushstrokes differently here than in her cottage studio. Better, maybe. Or just different. She couldn't tell anymore.

"The height's good." He adjusted the frame a fraction to the left. "Want to check the angle from where people will come into the room?"

She walked to the entrance and turned back. Three paintings in a row, telling a story she hadn't meant to tell. The lighthouse interior with its brass lamp and half-written letter. The storm-tossed seascape, all churning grays and desperate blues. The courtyard gathering, warm with community she'd only started to believe in.

"They look..." The words stuck. Professional? Real? Like they belonged here?

He joined her in the entryway. "They look like you. I mean, like your work. The real work, not the—"

"Not the stuff I did for Franklin." She finished the thought he was too polite to voice. "Yes, these are different."

Different because she'd painted them for herself.

Grant moved back to adjust the middle painting. His movements had changed over the past week as they'd prepared for the festival. Less careful. More fluid.

"You've been working." She nodded toward his hands, noting the small cuts and calluses that hadn't been there before.

He flexed his fingers, seeming surprised she'd noticed. "Just playing around. Found some good driftwood after that storm last weekend."

Playing around. Right. She'd seen him hauling materials into the back workshop, heard the sounds of sawing and sanding when she'd stopped by yesterday. He was creating again, even if he wouldn't call it that yet.

"Show me?" The request slipped out before she could stop it.

He hesitated. She recognized the look. The fear of being seen creating. Of someone witnessing the vulnerable act of making something from nothing.

"They're not..." He stopped. Started again. "They're just experiments."

She motioned toward her paintings. "So were these. Still are, really."

Something shifted in his expression. He led her through the gallery and back to his workshop, a space that smelled of sawdust and linseed oil and possibly hope, if hope really had a scent. Three small sculptures sat on the workbench. Driftwood and copper wire. Sea glass and rusted metal. Beautiful in their rawness.

"I started at my father's studio. Then… I just couldn't stop. I've been working here too."

She moved closer, studying how he'd balanced organic curves against angular metal. "These are wonderful."

"They're not like my New York work." His voice carried apology and defiance.

"No. They're better." She meant it. His earlier pieces had been clever and sophisticated. These had soul. "More honest."

He laughed, but it wasn't bitter. Just surprised. "Honest. Yeah, maybe that's it."

She reached out to touch one sculpture, then pulled back. "May I?"

"Sure." He picked it up and handed it to her.

The piece was lighter than she'd expected. Smooth wood against rough metal. It felt alive in her hands.

"You should include these in the festival." She set the sculpture down carefully.

"No." The word came fast and firm. "Not ready for that."

She understood. Wow, did she understand. But they each had to reach that decision in their own time. "Okay. But maybe soon?"

"Maybe." He was watching her with an expression she couldn't quite read. "Emily, I—"

The workshop suddenly felt smaller. Warmer. She was acutely aware of paint under her fingernails, the way the afternoon light caught in his hair, and how long it had been since she'd stood this close to anyone.

"We should probably..." She motioned vaguely toward the gallery.

"Right. The paintings. Make sure they're secure."

They returned to the festival space, but something had changed. The air between them crackled, like the atmosphere before a Gulf storm. She tried to focus on practical matters like the artist statement she'd finally agreed to write. But she kept getting distracted by the way Grant moved through his gallery and this festival room. Sure and graceful, like he belonged here.

Like maybe she was starting to belong here too.

"The statement's still too long. I sound like I'm defending a dissertation." She frowned at her notebook.

Grant read over her shoulder. Close enough that

she could smell his soap. Close enough that she had to concentrate on breathing normally.

"Cut the second paragraph?"

She crossed out the offending section. Better. Cleaner. Like everything else she'd been learning here, sometimes less was more honest than more.

She set the pen down. "There, three paintings and one short statement. Officially ready for public consumption." She looked directly at him. "I'm still worried about Julian, though. What he might do. If he'll show up."

"I know." He reached out and covered her hand with his. "But I'm so proud of you. I swear, you're the strongest woman I've ever met."

The warmth of his touch traveled up her arm. When had simple contact started feeling so significant?

She turned her hand palm up, letting their fingers interlock. "I don't feel strong." She shrugged. "But I'm tired of hiding."

She squeezed his hand, then let go before she could do something stupid. Like step closer. Like find out if his lips were as warm as his hands. "We should test the lighting. Make sure the paintings are visible from different angles."

For the next hour, they worked side by side. Adjusting spotlights. Measuring distances. Avoiding each other and the growing tension that made every accidental touch feel deliberate.

"Try now," Grant called from behind the desk where the lighting controls lived.

She studied her paintings under the new configuration. The lighthouse interior glowed. The seascape looked properly turbulent. The courtyard scene felt inviting.

"Perfect." She turned to tell him and found him closer than expected.

Much closer.

"Sorry, I was just—" He started to step back.

"Grant…"

They stood there, caught in the space between stepping forward and stepping back. Her heart hammered.

This was such a bad idea. She'd come here to hide, to heal, and to figure out who she was without scandal defining her. Getting involved with anyone, especially someone who understood her damage so well, could complicate everything.

But when Grant's hand came up to brush a strand of hair from her face, every sensible thought evaporated.

"Emily." The way he said her name made it sound new, sound special.

She leaned in, or maybe he did, or maybe they both moved at once. Then his lips were on hers, gentle and sure, and she was kissing him back like she'd been wanting to for weeks.

The gallery, the paintings, and the festival all

faded away. There was just this. The warmth of his mouth. The solid feel of his chest under her hands. The rightness of it, despite all the reasons it shouldn't feel right.

When they finally pulled apart, her head spun. Grant looked equally stunned.

"I..." He cleared his throat. "I didn't plan that."

"Me neither." She touched her lips, still feeling the echo of contact. "Grant, I don't know if I can—"

He stepped back, giving her space. "I know. We both have reasons to be careful."

Careful. Right. Except she'd been careful for two years, and where had it gotten her? Alone in a cottage, afraid to paint, afraid to connect, afraid to live.

"I like you." The words tumbled out before she could stop them. "More than I expected to. More than is probably smart. But I don't know if I'm ready for... whatever this is."

"I like you too." He gave her a lopsided smile. "And I'm probably not ready either. But maybe we don't have to be ready. Maybe we just have to be willing to see what happens."

She considered this. In her old life, she'd planned everything. Calculated every move. Look how well that had worked out.

"One day at a time?" She offered.

He nodded. "I can do that."

CHAPTER 23

Emily reached for her coffee cup. The morning crowd at Harbor Brew buzzed with its usual energy as fishermen grabbed their daily caffeine before heading to the docks. Locals caught up on town gossip, and tourists asked for directions to the lighthouse. She'd started coming here most mornings, drawn by the warmth and the way people had begun to nod at her in recognition.

Not quite belonging, but no longer invisible either.

"Emily Shaw."

The voice cut through the comfortable chatter like glass breaking. Her hand froze halfway to her cup. She knew that voice. Had heard it in her nightmares for months after everything fell apart in Chicago.

Julian Holloway stood three feet from her table.

His expensive suit didn't belong here. Neither did he. His face hadn't changed since the courtroom. Same tight jaw. Same eyes that said he was the wronged party.

"I wondered how long it would take you to crawl out from whatever hole you'd been hiding in. Imagine my surprise when I saw your name attached to an art exhibition. Still trading on my father's reputation, I see." His voice carried across the shop. Conversations died.

The familiar paralysis gripped her, the same frozen inability to defend herself that had made the Chicago situation so much worse. She'd practiced what she might say if this moment ever came, but all those imagined speeches evaporated.

"I'm not—" The words stuck. "Your father asked me to help."

"My father was dying. Vulnerable. And you took advantage of that vulnerability to steal his legacy." Julian stepped closer. Several customers shifted uncomfortably. Sally Morris, at the next table, held her coffee cup midway up to her lips.

"That's not what happened." It annoyed her that her voice sounded weak and uncertain. Why couldn't she sound stronger? Why did his presence still reduce her to this?

"No? Then explain why his final works suddenly showed techniques he'd never used before. Why the brushwork changed. Why the color palettes shifted."

Julian's voice rose with each accusation. "You couldn't wait for him to die before putting your mark on his masterpieces."

"He asked me to finish them. He gave me his sketches, his notes—"

"Convenient that a dying man would hand over his artistic legacy to his student. Even more convenient that you were the only witness to these supposed conversations."

She felt every eye in the coffee shop on her, felt them watching. This was Chicago all over again, with the public humiliation and the inability to make anyone understand the truth when lies sounded so much more dramatic.

"The court cleared me." She hated how defensive she sounded.

"The court said there wasn't enough evidence to prosecute. That's not the same as innocent." Julian pulled out his phone, and Emily recognized the gesture. He was recording. "I'm here to inform you that I'll be filing a new lawsuit. You will not exhibit any artwork in this town or anywhere else. You will not profit from your continued exploitation of the Holloway name."

"I'm not using his name. These are my paintings—"

"Painted with techniques you learned from my father. Using his methods. Trading on the reputation you built while hiding in his shadow." He leaned down, his face inches from hers. "You think moving to some fishing town changes anything? That I'd let you start over like nothing happened?"

Her hands shook. Coffee sloshed over the rim of her cup. Someone moved behind Julian. She barely registered it. All she saw was Julian's angry face and the phone recording her humiliation.

"That's enough." Grant's voice was steel. He stepped between them, forcing Julian to back up. "You need to leave."

Julian's eyes flicked to Grant, assessing. "And you are?"

"The owner of the gallery showing Emily's work. Also someone who doesn't appreciate bullies harassing people in public." Grant's shoulders were rigid. "I said leave."

"I see." Julian's smile turned predatory. "Then you should know you're about to feature a fraud in your exhibition. I hope your gallery has good lawyers."

"As a matter of fact, we do." Grant didn't move. "We have all these witnesses of you harassing and threatening one of our own. Florida has excellent stalking laws."

"This isn't over." Julian tucked his phone away. His gaze found Emily again over Grant's shoulder. "You can't hide behind small-town protectors forever. I'll make sure everyone knows exactly what you are."

He strode out, leaving shocked silence in his wake. She stared at the coffee pooling on her table, unable to lift her eyes. She couldn't look up. Couldn't make herself meet anyone's eyes. All these weeks of slowly building connections, of starting to feel safe, and Julian had destroyed it in minutes.

"Emily." Grant's voice was gentle now. His hand touched her shoulder.

She flinched away. "Don't."

"Let me help—"

"I need to go." She stood abruptly, her chair scraping against the floor. Everyone was still staring. Sally Morris looked sympathetic, but others wore expressions of curiosity or judgment. By noon, the entire town would know about the scene.

Emily fled.

She made it halfway down the block before Grant caught up. "Emily, wait."

"Why?" She whirled on him. "So you can tell me it's going to be okay? That Julian's just blowing smoke? I've been through this before, Grant. He won't stop. He has money and anger and all the time in the world to destroy my life."

"So you're going to let him?"

The question stopped her cold. "Let him?"

"Run? Hide? Give up on the exhibition? Give him exactly what he wants?" Grant's jaw was tight. "Is that the plan?"

"You don't understand—"

"I understand better than you think." He stepped closer. Not crowding her, just closing the distance. "I understand what it's like to have someone try to destroy everything you've built. To make you doubt your own talent and worth."

Her anger deflated. Of course, he understood. Miranda. The gallery betrayal. He'd lived his own version of this nightmare.

"But I actually might have done something wrong." The admission slipped out before she could stop it. "What if Julian's right? What if I did unconsciously steal from Franklin? What if I can't tell anymore where his influence ends and my voice begins?"

"Then we figure it out together." Grant's certainty steadied her. "But we don't let him win by default. We don't give up before the fight starts."

"He'll drag your gallery into this. He'll try to destroy your reputation too."

"Let him try." Something fierce flashed in Grant's eyes. "I'm not Daniel, Emily. I'm not going to walk away because things get difficult."

The comparison to her ex-husband should have stung. Instead, it felt like recognition. Grant saw her patterns, her expectations of abandonment, and was deliberately choosing differently.

"I need to think." She wrapped her arms around herself. "I need—"

He stepped back, giving her space. "Time. I

know. But don't think too long. The festival is in three days. Your paintings are hung. The story they tell is powerful and real and has nothing to do with Franklin Holloway."

She wanted to believe him. But Julian's voice echoed in her head, mixing with all the old accusations until she couldn't separate truth from lies anymore.

"I'll call you later." She turned away before he could respond.

The walk back to the lighthouse felt endless. Every person she passed seemed to be staring, though she knew most of them hadn't been in the coffee shop. Paranoia and history blurred together. By the time she reached Starfish Cottage, she was practically running.

Inside, she locked the door and leaned against it. Her paintings of the lighthouse interior, the storm-tossed seascape, and the warm courtyard gathering. Had she unconsciously channeled Franklin's techniques into them? Was there any part of her art that was purely her own?

The questions chased each other in circles. She sank onto her couch and pulled her knees to her chest. Maybe she should pack now. Leave before the festival. Save Grant the embarrassment of being associated with her scandal.

CHAPTER 24

A day later, Grant stared at the group of artists crowding his gallery's back room. Their faces wore expressions ranging from concern to outright hostility. He'd called this emergency meeting after three panicked phone calls and a string of texts, all sparked by Julian Holloway's coffee shop performance.

"I'm not displaying my work next to a fraud. That scene yesterday? The whole town's talking about it." Steven Chester crossed his arms. His coastal landscapes had been gallery staples for two years.

"Since when do we let strangers dictate who belongs in our community?" Grant kept his voice steady despite the anger building inside him.

"Since that stranger might sue us all for being

associated with stolen work." Missy Waters adjusted her glasses. Her silverwork brought in steady sales. "I can't afford lawyers, Grant."

"There's no stolen work." He scanned the room. Twelve artists. His gallery's backbone. "Emily was cleared of all charges."

"Legally cleared isn't the same as innocent." Steven echoed Julian's words.

"I know Emily's work. What she's showing has nothing to do with Franklin Holloway."

"How can you be sure? You've known her, what, a month or so?" This came from Dave Park, whose wood carvings occupied prime floor space.

"I know art. I know the difference between influence and imitation. Between learning from a master and stealing from one."

"Do you?" Missy's tone sharpened. "Or are you thinking with something other than your professional judgment?"

The room went silent. He felt the accusation hit its mark, but he didn't flinch.

"I'm thinking about what this gallery stands for. What we've built together." He looked at each of them. "We show real work. That's supposed to mean something."

Steven shook his head. "Pretty words. But they won't pay my mortgage if this gallery gets dragged through legal battles."

"Then go." Grant motioned to the door. "If you're here for guaranteed safety and easy sales, you're in the wrong place."

Several artists shifted uncomfortably. The irony of the situation wasn't lost on Grant. He'd built this gallery as a safe haven for local artists, and now he was challenging that very safety.

"That's not fair. We've supported this gallery through thin times. We deserve to protect ourselves." Dave shook his head.

He softened slightly. "You're right. You do. But protection can't come at the cost of our integrity. The moment we let outside threats determine whose work we show, we lose everything that makes us different from every other commercial gallery."

"Easy for you to say. Some of us are one bad month from bankruptcy." Missy gathered her purse.

She headed for the door. Steven followed. Then Dave. He watched them go, his stomach sinking. These weren't just business associates. They were friends. Community members he'd supported for years.

The remaining artists looked uncertain. Beth Ramsey, whose watercolors captured Starlight Shores' subtle beauty, spoke first. "I'm staying. That young woman paints the lighthouse like she understands it. I don't care what some Chicago lawyer thinks."

"Same." Jim, who kept a constant supply of pottery at the gallery, added. "I won't be party to running from a bully."

The others murmured agreement, but Grant knew he'd be hurt by the artists who left. The financial math was brutal and immediate. Artists pulling their work meant empty walls, lost commissions, and reduced foot traffic during the festival.

After they left, Grant sat in his empty gallery doing calculations. The numbers mocked him. Without those main artists, and if Julian did anything to ruin the traffic to the gallery from the festival, he'd have to dig deep into his savings just to cover next month's utilities. The careful balance he'd maintained for years was shattered.

His phone buzzed. A text from Miranda, of all people. *Heard you're having gallery troubles. I could find you a buyer. Think about it.*

Gossip spread quickly in the art world. He deleted the message without responding, but the timing made him want to throw his phone through the window.

He walked through his gallery, noting the gaps where artwork would be removed tomorrow. Missy's silverwork section. Steven's landscapes that tourists loved. Dave's wood carvings had become gallery signatures. The space would look abandoned. Depleted.

Was Emily worth this? The question came before he could stop it. Just weeks of knowing her against years of building this gallery. The math should be simple.

But he remembered her face in the coffee shop. The way Julian had reduced her to nothing with practiced cruelty.

No. Emily was worth it. Her paintings were worth it. The principle was worth it.

His phone rang. Sally Morris.

"Grant Stone, what's this I hear about artists pulling out of the festival?"

"It's handled, Sally."

"Is it? That poor girl was ambushed in Harbor Brew. And now your artists are punishing her for it?" Sally's indignation crackled through the phone. "You need help?"

"I need artists with spines." The bitterness leaked through despite his efforts.

"You need community support. Let me make some calls. There are more artists in this town than just your gallery roster."

"Sally—"

"Don't Sally me. That Holloway man was a bully, plain and simple. We don't let bullies win in Starlight Shores."

She hung up before he could respond. Grant smiled despite everything. Sally Morris was a force of nature when roused to action.

He returned to his calculations, trying to find a way to make the numbers work. Maybe if he cut his own draw completely. Delayed the roof repairs another year. Stopped the weekly artist workshops that barely broke even anyway.

Each cut felt like retreating. Giving Julian Holloway exactly what he wanted—Emily's isolation and Grant's gallery diminished.

No. He wouldn't let that happen. There had to be another way.

Grant stood and walked past the festival exhibit. The one that would have to be reworked with the artists pulling out. He looked at Emily's paintings. The lighthouse keeper's quarters that had moved Winnie to tears. The storm-tossed seascape that pulled the viewer into the actual storm. The courtyard gathering that radiated warmth and belonging.

They were good paintings. That should be enough. They deserved to be seen, regardless of one man's vendetta.

He was studying the brushwork—distinctly Emily's, nothing like the Franklin Holloway pieces he'd researched—when he noticed the envelope. His name was written across it in Emily's careful handwriting.

Inside, a single sheet of paper:

I heard what the artists said. Grant, I can't let my past

destroy what you've built. I'm leaving town. Take down my paintings. I'm sorry. Please don't try to find me. - Emily

The paper crumpled in his fist. She was running. Again. Letting Julian win without even fighting.

Grant grabbed his keys. No way she was leaving. Not without talking to him first.

CHAPTER 25

Emily folded another shirt and placed it in her suitcase. The familiar motion brought no comfort. How many times had she packed like this? Running from Chicago and the whispers and stares. Running from herself.

Her hands shook as she reached for her paint-stained jeans. The ones she'd worn that first morning on the beach when she'd finally found the courage to paint again. Just weeks ago, though it felt like a lifetime.

A knock at the door made her freeze.

"Emily? It's Winnie."

Of course it was. Winnie seemed to have a radar for when her tenants needed her most. Emily considered not answering, but that felt cowardly. More cowardly than running, somehow.

She opened the door. Winnie stood there with

no tea tray, no muffins, no pretense of a casual visit. Just those sharp green eyes that saw too much.

"Going somewhere?"

Emily let her in. "I have to. Julian won't stop. He'll destroy Grant's gallery, turn the whole town against me—"

"The whole town? Or just the frightened parts of it?"

"Does it matter? Grant already lost half his artists because of me."

"Because of their own fear. There's a difference."

Emily perched on the couch's edge, ready to bolt even in her own space. Winnie settled beside her.

"You know that my ancestors were sometimes very secretive, right?"

She nodded. There was always more to Winnie's stories.

"The town council didn't know the truth but wanted my grandfather removed as lighthouse keeper. Said he was bringing shame to Starlight Shores, making them all look like criminals." Winnie smiled. "My grandmother told them if they removed Henry, they'd have to find another keeper willing to work for the pittance they paid. In a storm. In the dark. While they sat safe in their warm houses."

"What happened?"

Winnie took Emily's hand. "Nothing. Because

when push came to shove, they needed the lighthouse more than they needed their righteousness. The point is, they backed down."

"This is different. I might actually have—"

"What? Learned from your mentor? Used techniques he taught you? Since when is that theft? Every artist builds on what came before. Every lighthouse keeper learned from the one who held the post before them."

A rapid knock interrupted them. Emily opened the door to find Melissa, camera bag slung over her shoulder.

"Good, you're still here." Melissa pushed past her. "I thought you might rabbit."

"I'm not rabbiting. I'm making a strategic retreat."

"Well, that man at Harbor Brew was a jerk. Don't let him get to you." Melissa nodded toward the open suitcase. "You should stay. Stand up to the bully."

Another knock. Sally Morris entered without waiting for permission, followed by Clint.

"Good gracious, it's like Grand Central in here." Sally surveyed the half-packed suitcase with obvious disapproval. "You're not letting that awful man run you out of town."

"I'm trying to protect—"

"Yourself?" Sally snorted. "Honey, I hid from

my first husband's family for six years. Know what it got me? An ulcer and a twitch."

"No, I'm trying to protect Grant and his gallery and the artists here."

"I think you should take a stand. Bullies like that Julian fellow need to be taught a lesson." Sally shook her head. "And Grant is a big boy. He'll figure out what to do about his gallery."

Clint stood awkwardly by the door. He finally cleared his throat. "Sally's right. About taking a stand."

Everyone turned to stare. Clint rarely spoke, let alone offered opinions on personal matters. "That Holloway guy is like the developers. Throwing weight around. Trying to force his version of truth on everyone." He met Emily's gaze. "You stay and fight, I'll make sure he doesn't bother you on the property."

She blinked back tears. Clint, who barely tolerated anyone, was offering protection.

Sally pulled out her phone. "I have lawyer friends in Tallahassee. One specializes in defamation cases. Shut down three similar harassment campaigns last year."

"But the festival—"

"Will go on." Winnie stood. "With you or without you. But I'd prefer it with you. Those paintings deserve to be seen."

"Grant's gallery—"

"Will survive. He's tougher than you think." Winnie moved to the door. "The question is, are you?"

They filed out, leaving Emily alone with her half-packed life. She sank onto the couch. Her phone buzzed with texts.

Beth from the gallery offering support: *Don't listen to the naysayers. Your work is remarkable and stands on its own merit. Don't let them chase you out of town. I'm on your side.*

Jan from Harbor Brew: *Free coffee tomorrow morning. My treat. That awful man isn't welcome in my shop again.*

When had she gained so many allies?

She looked around the cottage that had become home. The shells lining her windowsill. The sketchbooks scattered on every surface. The studio door standing open, no longer locked against her fears.

This wasn't Chicago. She wasn't sure when that had started to matter.

Her suitcase mocked her. How easy to zip it shut. Disappear. Start over somewhere else where Julian couldn't find her.

Except she'd already started over. Here. With paint-stained hands, tentative friendships, and walls that were finally coming down.

A car door slammed outside. Footsteps pounded

up her path. Grant burst through her unlocked door, chest heaving.

"No. You can't leave."

She stood slowly and studied his panicked face. His hair was wilder than usual. Paint smudged his shirt.

"You're too late."

"Emily—"

"No, you're too late to convince me to stay." She gestured around the room at the abandoned suitcase and the unpacked clothes. "Winnie and so many people in town already have."

Understanding flashed across his face. He crossed the room in two strides and scooped her up, twirling her around. Her startled laugh echoed off the walls.

"You're staying." Not a question. Pure relief.

"I'm staying." Her feet found the floor again, but his arms remained around her. "Julian can do his worst. I'm tired of running."

"Good." Grant pulled back enough to see her face. "Because I already told the remaining artists you have the prime spot at the festival. Would've been awkward to explain your empty wall space."

"Always so practical."

"Someone has to be." His thumb brushed her cheek. "You artists are all emotion and impulsive."

"Says the man who just burst through my door."

"I knocked. Mostly."

"You didn't."

"I *thought* about knocking."

She laughed again. When had laughter become so easy? "Thank you. For defending me at Harbor Brew. And today, when you had a bit of an artists' mutiny."

"Thank you for staying. For being brave enough to fight."

"I'm not brave."

"No?" Grant tilted his head. "Then what do you call this?"

"Tired of being afraid." She leaned into his warmth. "Winnie said sometimes we need to take a stand."

"Wise woman."

"The wisest." Emily looked up at him. "Kiss me?"

His lips met hers. Gentle. Sure. Outside, a car passed on the coastal road. The suitcase sat open on the floor, already looking like it belonged to someone else.

CHAPTER 26

Emily stared at the stack of papers Margaret Stone had spread across Winnie's kitchen table. Grant sat next to his mother as Margaret sorted documents into neat stacks, each one tabbed and highlighted.

"I've always been good at research. Thirty years as a librarian teaches you to spot inconsistencies." Margaret adjusted her reading glasses and tapped a highlighted passage.

The kitchen smelled of Winnie's fresh coffee and something cinnamon baking in the oven. Normal, comforting scents that made the documents feel even more surreal.

"Julian Holloway claimed you manipulated his father in his final months. But look at these dates." Margaret's voice stayed neutral, presenting facts rather than judgment.

Emily leaned forward. The timeline Margaret had constructed showed Emily's work schedule at the school.

"You were teaching full-time during most of the period Julian references." Margaret pointed to another column. "These are your class schedules, faculty meeting minutes, even parking garage records. You couldn't have been spending excessive time with Franklin when you were demonstrably elsewhere."

Margaret had done this for her. This woman she barely knew had spent hours—maybe days—piecing together evidence.

"There's more. Julian's initial accusations came six months after his father's death, right after the estate valuation showed Franklin's final works were worth considerably more than expected."

Grant moved closer, his hand finding Emily's shoulder. She leaned into it as Margaret continued.

"The timing suggests financial motivation rather than genuine concern about artistic integrity. A son who rarely visited his father suddenly becoming protective of his legacy? Only after learning its monetary value?"

She remembered those awful months and the shock of Julian's accusations. The way her colleagues had distanced themselves. Daniel's cold announcement that he wanted a divorce and needed to protect his career.

Margaret produced a photocopy of a handwritten note. "I also found this. Franklin's letter to the Art Institute, dated three months before his death. He specifically requested you as his collaborator and outlined exactly what he wanted you to complete."

Emily read Franklin's familiar scrawl twice before the words registered. *My dear student Emily has the skill and sensitivity to finish what my failing body cannot. This is my wish, freely given.*

"Julian would have received copies of all estate documents." Winnie leaned over the table. "He knew about this letter."

Grant's jaw tightened. "He knew and lied anyway. He destroyed your reputation, knowing you had done exactly what his father asked."

Margaret gathered the papers. "I've made copies of everything. If Julian persists with his threats, any competent lawyer could use this to counter his claims."

"I'm not sure why your lawyer didn't find all this before." Grant frowned.

"I didn't have the funds to get a top-notch lawyer, and I'm not sure my lawyer believed in my innocence anyway." She touched the photocopied letter. Franklin had been so careful to document everything, trying to protect her even then. He knew his son.

"Why did you do all this?" Her voice came out rough.

"Because I've seen enough unfair fights to know one when I see it." Margaret paused, then smiled. "And because my son hasn't looked at anyone the way he looks at you since—well, in a very long time."

Heat crept up Emily's neck. Grant squeezed her shoulder.

"So, what do you want to do with this information?" Margaret straightened the folders. "You could send copies to the Chicago papers that ran the original story. Clear your name publicly."

Emily winced at the thought of more attention, more scrutiny, and more people picking apart her life.

"Or you could simply keep it as protection. Sometimes the best weapon is one you never have to use." Winnie poured them all fresh coffee.

Margaret accepted the coffee with a grateful nod. "Julian's betting you'll do what you did before. Run." She shrugged. "Different situation now. You're not alone."

She looked around the kitchen. Grant beside her. His mother, who had no reason to help her. Winnie, refilling coffee like this was any normal morning.

"I don't want to drag you all into this mess."

"Too late." Grant's thumb traced gentle circles on her shoulder. "We're already here."

"The festival opens tomorrow." Winnie's eyes held that knowing look. "And this town's already made up its mind about you. Might as well accept it."

Margaret stood and patted Emily's hand. "Anyway, it's all there if you need it."

After she left, Emily sat staring at the folders filled with evidence of her innocence and proof that she had honored Franklin's wishes.

CHAPTER 27

Emily stood at the gallery's entrance, adjusting her skirt for the third time. The Springtide Festival banners fluttered in the morning breeze. Crowds had already gathered along the waterfront, their voices carrying across the courtyard.

"Ready?" Grant touched her elbow.

She nodded, not trusting her voice. The last time she'd shown her work publicly, everything had fallen apart. Chicago felt like a lifetime ago. Yet the fear remained. She caught herself checking for exits.

Inside the back gallery room, her three paintings commanded the prime wall. The lighthouse interior, the stormy seascape, and the courtyard gathering told a story she hadn't intended to write. They told a story about running and what happens when you stop.

"They look good." Grant's voice held quiet pride.

They did look good. Better than good. The lighting he'd adjusted yesterday—yet again—brought out subtleties in the brushwork.

The first visitors trickled in. She couldn't help herself as she braced against the possibility of Julian showing up. Luckily, a couple from Pensacola studied the painting of the lighthouse interior. She forced herself to stay near the paintings instead of hiding in the back office like she wanted.

"The detail in the brass work is extraordinary." The woman leaned closer. "You can almost feel the weight of that lamp."

"Thank you."

"Are you the artist?"

That simple question. Once, it would have filled her with pride. Then shame. Now... something in between.

"Yes."

"This reminds me of my grandfather's stories. He was a lighthouse keeper up near Mobile. You've captured something real here. The loneliness, but also the purpose."

The woman's husband nodded. "The brushwork in the storm piece. Those whites against the deep grays. How did you achieve that texture?"

Emily found herself explaining her technique. Layering. Scraping back. Building the paint like the weather itself. The man listened intently, asking follow-up questions that showed real understanding.

More visitors arrived. A steady stream now. She answered questions about historical research, about the lighthouse's architecture, and about her choice of colors. No one asked about Chicago. No one mentioned scandals or stolen legacies.

They saw the work. Just the work.

Yet, she couldn't help glancing toward the door. The threat of Julian clung to her.

"Your new pieces are causing quite a stir." Beth Ramsey appeared at her elbow, beaming. "I heard two collectors asking Grant about prices."

Prices. She'd actually agreed to sell them. Another step toward being a real artist again.

Sally Morris bustled through the crowd, her voice carrying. "Of course, you need to see Emily's paintings. She's captured our lighthouse like no one else has. Even Winnie got emotional when she saw them."

Suddenly, the crowd parted near the entrance.

There he was.

Julian Holloway stood in the doorway, his expression calculating as he scanned the gallery. His pressed suit and polished shoes looked out of place among the casual festival-goers.

Grant stepped closer to her side. "I've got this."

She held up a hand. "No. I'm not hiding anymore."

Julian's gaze found her paintings, and his eyes flashed. He moved through the crowd with deliberate purpose, stopping in front of the lighthouse interior. The same painting that had moved Winnie to tears.

"Interesting technique. Very reminiscent of a certain other artist's work." His voice carried just loud enough for nearby visitors to hear.

Emily's hands clenched, but she forced them to relax. The couple from Pensacola glanced between them, confusion flickering across their faces.

"Actually," the woman said, "I was just thinking how unique the style is. My grandfather was a lighthouse keeper, and this captures something I've never seen in maritime art before."

Julian's smile didn't reach his eyes. "Yes, well, some people are very good at... appropriation."

"That's enough." Grant moved forward, but Emily caught his arm.

"Sir, are you an art critic?" A young man with a notebook stepped closer. A journalist or podcaster, probably, covering the festival.

Julian straightened his tie. "I have some expertise in identifying authentic work versus—"

"Because I teach at SCAD—Savannah College of Art and Design." The young man pointed at Emily's storm painting. "What strikes me about these pieces is how honest they feel. The way the paint builds in layers and creates depth through texture rather than just color. It's actually quite innovative."

Heat crept up Julian's neck. More people gathered, drawn by the discussion. Emily recognized the danger in their attention, but also something else. They were looking at her work, not at Julian.

"The historical research alone is impressive." An older woman Emily recognized from the historical society stepped forward. "I've been documenting the lighthouse for forty years, and she's captured details I've only seen in archival photographs."

"Details can be copied," Julian said, but his voice had lost some of its conviction.

"Not like this." Grant's mother appeared through the crowd, Margaret Stone in full librarian mode. "This level of architectural accuracy combined with emotional interpretation? That takes both skill and intuition."

Sally Morris's voice carried from near the courtyard painting. "Oh, Emily, someone's asking about commissioning a painting of their family's old fishing cottage. Should I send them over?"

The redirect was obvious but effective. The crowd's attention shifted from Julian to the possibility of custom work. Emily caught Sally's wink and felt a surge of gratitude.

"I'd be happy to discuss commissions after the festival." She surprised herself with how normal she sounded.

Julian stood isolated now, the crowd flowing around him toward the paintings. His face reddened as people continued discussing technique and historical accuracy, their enthusiasm genuine and unforced. He walked over to her and leaned in close. "Enjoy your little moment while you can."

A man with paint-stained fingers interrupted them. "The way you've captured light reflecting off brass. Are you using a glazing technique?"

She turned to the man. "Actually, it's direct painting, but I work the metallic elements while the base layer is still tacky. It creates a different kind of luminosity."

The painter nodded eagerly. "Would you mind if I tried something similar? I've been struggling with reflective surfaces."

They talked technique while Julian faded into the background. When she glanced back, he was gone.

At least for now.

"Look at Grant's sculptures." Beth's voice drew Emily's attention to the corner where Grant had finally agreed to display his new work. A small crowd gathered around the driftwood and metal pieces.

The sculptures were raw and honest, nothing like his sophisticated New York pieces. These spoke of storms weathered, of things broken and reformed. They complemented her paintings in unexpected ways—his three-dimensional interpretations of the same forces she'd captured in paint.

"They're talking to each other." The SCAD instructor moved between Grant's sculptures and her paintings. "Are you two collaborating? These feel like they're talking to each other."

Grant caught her eye across the room.

"We didn't plan it," she said. "But we've been walking the same beaches, watching the same lighthouse."

The festival sounds washed over her, filled with conversations about art, not scandal, and questions about technique, not accusations. Her work stood on its own merit, speaking its own truth.

As the festival wound down, they headed for the lighthouse for what Emily found out was the annual first night of the Springtide Festival dinner. The cottage residents and friends gathered to celebrate.

Emily stepped into the courtyard, where string lights crisscrossed overhead, their warm glow competing with the sunset painting the Gulf in shades of coral and gold. She carried a plate of Sally's famous crab cakes while Winnie directed the placement of tables with the precision of a general organizing troops. "The beverage station goes there, Clint. No, there. Where people can access it without blocking the garden path." Winnie's voice carried affectionate exasperation.

Emily set down the crab cakes and surveyed the growing spread. Jan from Harbor Brew had contributed several thermoses of coffee and her special lemon bars. The Sandpiper had sent over platters of fresh seafood.

Grant appeared at her elbow. "Your paintings sold. All three. The couple from Pensacola bought the storm painting, and a collector from Tampa wants the courtyard scene."

"And the lighthouse?"

"It sold too."

Sold. Not just displayed or tolerated, but valued enough that strangers would take them home. Would live with them. "I haven't sold anything in years." The admission slipped out before she could stop it.

"Then it's about time." His hand found the small of her back, warm and steady.

Melissa emerged from her cottage carrying her camera. She hesitated at the edge of the courtyard as she often did at gatherings. Emily caught her eye and waved her over. "Document this?" Emily gestured at the controlled chaos of setup. "Winnie's been organizing this courtyard for decades. It's its own kind of art."

Melissa's shoulders relaxed. Having a purpose always helped. "The light's perfect right now. That golden hour glow against the lighthouse." As if summoned by the mention of light, the lighthouse beam flickered on. Still an hour before true darkness, but Winnie always lit it early on celebration nights. The beam swept across the courtyard, a familiar constant rhythm.

"Speech time." Sally clinked a spoon against her wine glass. "Winnie, you start."

"I don't make speeches." Winnie smoothed her apron, but Emily caught the pleased flush in her cheeks. "I just want to say how proud I am of our artists today. Grant and Emily both showed work that took courage to create and even more courage to share."

"To our artists," someone called out.

"To selling paintings," Sally added, raising her glass of sweet tea as everyone laughed.

Emily found herself surrounded by faces that had become familiar over the past weeks. Sally, who'd staunchly defended her. Jan, who'd banned Julian from the coffee shop. Clint, who'd offered protection in his gruff way.

"I should thank everyone." Emily's words tumbled out. "When I came here, I was just looking for somewhere to hide. But you all gave me something better. A place to belong."

Winnie reached over and squeezed her hand. "The lighthouse has a way of keeping people here. We just helped it along."

CHAPTER 28

The last day of the festival, Emily's hands trembled slightly as she arranged her notes at the panel table. The festival tent buzzed with conversation. She'd agreed to this discussion about "Art and Community" weeks ago, before Julian's threats and before she knew he'd follow her here.

"Our next question comes from the audience." The moderator scanned the raised hands.

Julian stood in the third row. Of course he did.

"I'd like to ask Ms. Shaw about artistic integrity. Specifically about artists who exploit dying mentors for personal gain." His voice carried that familiar edge of righteousness.

The tent went silent. Her breath caught, but she kept her eyes on Julian. No more running. No more letting him control the narrative.

"Are you asking about my work with your father,

Julian? Because I'd be happy to discuss that." She kept her voice steady.

His jaw clenched. "I'm asking about fraud. About signing your name to another artist's work."

Grant shifted in his chair beside her. She touched his arm lightly. This was her fight. "Your father asked me to complete three paintings in his final months." Emily pulled Margaret's folder from her bag. "I have his written request here, along with documentation of every session we worked together."

"You manipulated a dying man—"

"I was teaching full-time." She opened the folder. "These are my class schedules, faculty meeting attendance records, and even parking receipts. I spent exactly twelve documented sessions with Franklin, all at his request."

Julian's face flushed. "You can't prove—"

"I have his written request. It's—here." She fumbled with the folder. "And documentation. I can prove everything. Including the fact that you first accused me of fraud six months after your father's death. Right after learning his final works had increased in value."

Murmurs rippled through the audience. She saw Sally in the front row, nodding encouragement.

"You're twisting this—"

"Your father wrote to the Art Institute three months before he died." Her voice gained strength.

"He specifically requested I complete his work. He outlined exactly what he wanted done. You received copies of all estate documents. You knew about this letter."

Julian's mouth opened and closed.

"You knew I was doing exactly what Franklin asked. You knew, and you destroyed my life anyway. Not because you cared about artistic integrity, but because you were angry. Angry that your father chose to spend his final months with me instead of you."

"You don't know anything about my relationship with my father."

The pain in his voice almost made her falter. Almost.

"I know Franklin talked about you constantly." She softened her tone. "He kept every article about your business success. He understood why you couldn't visit more. The distance, your work—"

"Stop." Julian's voice cracked.

"He loved you. He was proud of you. He kept a photo of you on his easel. Did you know that?"

Julian's hands clenched at his sides. The audience had gone completely quiet.

"He asked me to finish those paintings because his hands couldn't hold a brush anymore. Because he wanted his final vision completed. I did my best to honor that. I'm sorry you weren't there. I'm sorry you feel excluded from his final months. But that's not my fault." She set down the folder.

"You had no right—"

"I had every right." Her voice stayed calm. "Your father gave me that right. And I won't apologize for helping him anymore."

Someone in the audience started clapping. Then another. The sound built slowly, spreading through the tent.

Julian's face twisted. "This isn't over."

"Yes, it is." Grant stood beside her. "You've harassed Emily in multiple states now. If you contact her again, we'll file charges."

"We?" Julian's laugh had a bitter edge. "Let me guess. Another man fooled by her act."

"No. A man who recognizes truth when he sees it. Who knows what it costs to create authentic work. And who won't let bullies destroy good people."

More applause. Emily saw Winnie near the tent entrance, arms crossed, looking like she'd bet money on this exact outcome.

"You want to talk about exploitation?" An older woman stood in the fifth row. "My gallery dropped me after anonymous complaints about what they called my controversial work. Turned out to be a rival artist. These baseless accusations happen all the time."

"My nephew lost his teaching position over

fabricated plagiarism charges." A man called out. "The truth came out eventually, but the damage was done."

"That's—yes, these are important issues, but perhaps we should—" The moderator leaned into her microphone.

Julian backed toward the aisle. His grand confrontation had become something else entirely. A conversation about false accusations. About the cost of public shaming. About community support versus mob mentality.

"Julian," Emily called after him. He paused but didn't turn. "Your father's last painting. The sunset over water. He said it reminded him of a fishing trip you took together when you were twelve. He talked about that day all the time."

Julian's shoulders sagged. Then he was gone, pushing out of the tent into the afternoon sun, disappearing into the crowd.

Emily's legs buckled. She dropped into her chair, hands shaking now that the adrenaline was draining away. Not from fear, but from finally saying it all out loud.

The moderator was saying something about taking a break. People were standing, talking in clusters. The tent buzzed with energy, but it felt distant. Muffled.

"You okay?" Grant's hand found hers under the table, and his thumb brushed across her knuckles.

She squeezed his fingers and tried to answer, but no words came out.

"Come on." Grant stood, still holding her hand, and guided her toward the side exit of the tent.

Outside, a kid was screaming about dropped ice cream. Normal festival chaos. Grant led her around the back to an alley between buildings, away from the crowds and the glaring sun. She leaned against the side of a building and sucked in deep breaths.

"Hey." Grant stepped in front of her. "You with me?"

She nodded, still not trusting her voice.

"That was incredible." His hands came up to her shoulders, steady and warm. "What you did in there. Standing up to him. Emily, that was—"

"I was so scared." The words came out shaky. She laughed, but it sounded wrong.

"You didn't look scared. You looked fearless."

"I was terrified." She met his eyes finally. "But I was so tired of being afraid. So tired of letting him make me small."

Grant's hands slid down her arms. He didn't let go. "You're not small. You never were."

"I…" The words just wouldn't come to her.

He reached over and tilted up her face. "Emily. Look at me."

She did. His blue eyes were intense, certain.

"You are one of the most talented artists I've ever met. Your work has emotion and depth that most people spend their whole lives trying to achieve. Franklin saw that. I see it. Everyone who sees your paintings sees it."

She looked directly into his eyes. "You stayed." The words came out before she could stop them. "In there. You stayed beside me."

Grant's expression softened. "Of course I stayed."

"Daniel didn't. The scandal hit, and he filed for divorce within a month. Said he couldn't be associated with that kind of controversy. That he had an image to protect." The bitterness in her voice surprised her. "He didn't even ask if it was true. He just assumed I'd done something wrong and decided I wasn't worth the trouble."

Grant's jaw tightened. "Then he's a fool."

"Maybe. But I thought... I guess I thought that's what people do. When things get hard. When staying gets complicated."

"Some people." Grant's hands were still on her face, his gaze holding hers. "Not me."

"Why?"

"Why what?"

"Why stay? Why defend me? This could hurt your gallery. Your reputation. Why risk it?"

He was quiet for a moment, his thumb tracing a line across her cheekbones. "Because you got knocked down and you got back up. And you're still painting. That's—" He shook his head. "That's not nothing."

"Grant—"

"And maybe because I'm a little bit in love with the way you look at the ocean when you paint. Like you're having a conversation with it." A small smile tugged at his mouth. "Or the way you argue with me about composition. Or how you defend Melissa when you think someone's being dismissive of her work."

"You can't—"

"Can't what? Notice you? Care about you?" He leaned closer. "Too late."

She should probably say something. Do something other than stare at him like she'd forgotten how words worked.

"I'm a mess," she finally managed. "I'm still figuring out who I am after everything. I don't know if I'm ready for—"

"I'm not asking you to be ready. I'm just asking you to stop thinking you have to do this alone."

She exhaled. Actually exhaled, like she'd been holding her breath for months. "I found my voice again today."

"I heard." Pride filled his expression. "You were magnificent."

She looked down at their joined hands. His nails had paint under them. Cadmium yellow, maybe. She focused on that instead of looking at his face.

"Thank you," she said quietly. "For being there. For believing me."

"Always." He said it like a promise.

People were starting to drift around on the street. The break was probably ending soon. Real life returning. But standing here with Grant's hand in hers, Emily felt hope sweep through her. She felt good. Suspiciously good. The kind of good that used to scare her.

"We should go back," she said, but she didn't move.

"Probably." Grant didn't move either.

She smiled. "I have another panel in twenty minutes."

"Then we have nineteen minutes."

"To do what?"

He grinned. "Oh, I have plans for those nineteen minutes."

He leaned down then and kissed her gently. When he finally pulled back, she grinned up at him. "You make the best plans."

His lips curved into a wide smile. "I do, don't I?"

CHAPTER 29

A month later, Emily stood in Grant's office, trying to process the words he was saying. "You want me to what?"

"Be my partner in this new venture."

Grant leaned against the edge of the desk. "You don't have to decide right now. I know it's a lot to take in."

It was more than a lot. A month ago, she'd been ready to run from Starlight Shores forever. Now Grant was offering her this partnership.

"The Sanders Foundation wants to fund artist residencies? And they specifically requested my involvement?" She stared at him.

"Yeah, my mother is kind of remarkable when she sets her mind to something. She was determined to find a way to expand the teaching side of the gallery. She found the Sanders Foundation."

"Your mother doesn't do anything halfway."

"She's adopted you. Resistance is futile."

Emily smiled at that. After years of being rejected over the scandal, having Margaret Stone champion her cause felt like an unexpected gift.

"The foundation was impressed by your work at the festival. And it seems the art world is finally believing your story of what happened with Franklin. It's about time." His voice held that protective edge she'd grown to love. "The foundation thinks combining your teaching experience with the gallery space could create something special."

Special. Everything about the last few weeks had been special in ways that terrified her. The paintings she'd sold. The community that had rallied around her. The way Grant looked at her like she was worth fighting for.

"This would mean staying here in Starlight Shores." He looked directly at her.

"Yes, it would." She stood, walked to the window, and watched a pelican dive into the water as the first hints of sunset colored the sky. "I came here to hide. I thought if I just stayed quiet enough, small enough… I don't know. I thought maybe I could disappear."

"Emily—"

She held up a hand. "Let me finish."

He nodded.

"Then I started sketching again. Then painting. Met Winnie and Melissa and even Clint with all his rules." A laugh bubbled up, surprising her. "I painted that lighthouse like my life depended on it." She shrugged. "Because maybe it did."

She walked back to the desk and picked up the paperwork from the foundation. "Teaching workshops. Curating exhibitions. Building something that lasts. With you."

"We'd be good partners." Grant moved closer but didn't touch her. "We already are."

They were. Somehow, between hanging paintings and adjusting lights and sharing their broken pieces, they'd become a team. But this felt bigger. More permanent. More real.

"What about your current artists? Steven and Dave and a few others made their feelings pretty clear about associating with me."

"They've all asked to come back."

She reached out and took his hand. "You should let them. We all do… ah… unexpected things when we're scared."

"That's really what you want?"

"Yes." She squeezed his hand, then changed the subject. "So the teaching space would be in the back?"

"Yes, where we had the festival art. Melissa's already offered to teach photography workshops.

And Winnie has a whole list of artists she thinks would make good residents."

Of course, Winnie had a list. The woman had probably been planning this since Emily first showed up at her door, scared and convinced she'd never paint again.

She took a deep breath, set down the paperwork, and stepped into his arms. "Okay, yes. Let's do this."

He pulled back to look at her. "You're sure?"

"I'm sure I want to try. This town, these people, and you are worth the risk. And I'm tired of running."

He kissed her then, and Emily let herself believe in second chances, in new beginnings, and partnerships that might actually last.

When he finally stepped back, he smiled at her and took her hand. "I think we should go to the beach. That's where this all started."

"I think that's a great plan."

He led her through town, where countless locals called out greetings. They crossed over to the beach and headed toward the lighthouse. She thought about Winnie's words about promises kept and harbors found, and how some places called to the people who needed them most.

They continued walking along the shoreline as the waves rolled in and the sun started dipping below the horizon, tossing brilliant streaks of purple and orange across the sky. He held her hand in his, and it felt natural and right.

She finally stopped and looked directly at him. "You're sure about this partnership?"

"The gallery needs you." His hands framed her face. "But that's not why I want you as my partner."

"No?" Her heart skipped. The way he looked at her made her feel eighteen and eighty all at once. She felt ridiculous and grateful at the same time.

"I want to argue about where to hang paintings. I want—" He laughed at himself. "I want coffee breaks that turn into something else. I want this. With you."

"Grant—"

"I love you." His words came out sure and steady. "I think I started falling for you that morning on the beach when you were painting the lighthouse. Maybe before that."

She thought about all the reasons to be careful and all the ways love had failed her before. But standing here with the lighthouse keeping watch and the Gulf stretching endlessly before them, those fears felt as insubstantial as seafoam.

The lighthouse beam swept past. A promise and a blessing.

"I love you too." Her words felt like coming home. "I love your stubborn integrity and your protective heart. I love how you fight for this community. I love that you gave me a second chance when everyone else would have walked away."

Grant pulled her into a kiss full of new beginnings and permanent things. When they finally broke apart, he smiled. His whole face changed when he smiled like that.

"My mom is going to be insufferable." His grin widened. "She's been planning our partnership since she first met you."

"The gallery partnership?" Emily raised an eyebrow.

"Oh, she's got plans for that too." He pulled her close. "But I'm more interested in this one."

He kissed her again. Behind them, the lighthouse beam swept across the water and the waves kept coming in, steady as always.

The kettle began to whistle, a familiar, cheerful sound in the quiet of the keeper's quarters. Winnie moved from the window, where she'd been watching the last sunset spill across the Gulf. She poured the steaming water over tea leaves in her favorite ceramic pot. The scent of bergamot filled the kitchen.

The back door creaked open. She didn't need to turn to know who it was. Clint always entered that way, with a hesitation that suggested he was never quite sure of his welcome, even in the house where he'd spent half his childhood.

"There's tea if you want some." She set two mugs on the counter.

"Not staying." His voice was low, as usual. He stood in the doorway between the kitchen and the living room, holding a large, rectangular object wrapped in a simple brown blanket.

It was unusual for him to seek her out. Their interactions were mostly functional, centered on property maintenance and the needs of their tenants. "Everything all right?"

"Fine." He shifted his weight. "Got something for you. A present. I kept waiting for the perfect time to give it to you… but… now seemed good." He shrugged.

A present? The word felt foreign between them. They didn't exchange gifts, not since he was a boy and would bring her shells he'd found on the beach. She dried her hands on a dish towel and waited as he carried the object to the kitchen table. He unwrapped it carefully, his large, calloused hands surprisingly gentle.

It was Emily's painting of the lighthouse study.

Her grandfather's study.

She reached out, her fingers hovering just above the canvas, not daring to touch the textured surface. Emily had captured it all. Even the half-written letter, a detail that made Winnie's heart ache with the memories flooding through her.

She had thought the memory of that room would fade with her. That it would become just another ghost in a house full of them. But here it was, painted by a woman who had never even seen it.

"Grant said the collectors wanted all three paintings," Clint said quietly, watching her face. "I told him this one wasn't for sale. That it belonged here. He agreed with me."

She finally looked at him. "You bought it?"

He shrugged and dropped his gaze to the floor. "Figured it was the right thing to do."

Winnie closed the distance between them and wrapped her arms around his waist, burying her face in the rough fabric of his shirt. He stood stiffly for a moment, then his arms came around her in an awkward embrace. She held on. The painting was a gift, but Clint's understanding of why it mattered was the true present. He had seen what the painting represented. Not just art, but their history and their legacy.

She pulled back and smiled up at him. "Thank you, Clint. I never thought I'd see the painting again."

"It's just a painting, Aunt Win." His gruffness was a shield, she knew.

"No. It's more than that."

He nodded once, then retreated toward the door. "Got to check the lights in the courtyard. Saw one that was flickering." He was gone before she could say more, leaving her alone with the painting.

She carried the painting into the living room and propped it on the mantel. She moved a collection of old photographs to make room. It fit perfectly, as if it had always been meant to be there. The amber light from a nearby lamp made the painted brass of the oil lamp in the painting glow.

She sank into her armchair and just looked at the painting. All those secrets. The ones the men in her family had documented in the journal and the ones they'd taken to their graves. She wondered if she would ever piece the whole story together. If she was even meant to. Maybe some secrets were best left undisturbed.

I hope you enjoyed *Lighthouse Cottages*, the first book in the Starlight Shores series. I'm really enjoying writing about Winnie. She'll be an important character in all the books in the series. Next up is *Harbor Festival*, because, you know me, I love to put festivals and small-town gatherings in my books. In *Harbor Festival*, you'll meet Cassidy, a burned-out marketing executive staying at Heron Cottage at the lighthouse. And, of course, there will be more of Winnie and the mystery surrounding the history of the lighthouse.

Each time I sit down to write, I'm reminded of all of you who have embraced my stories of love and community. I hope you've found a bit of home in these pages.

As always, thanks for reading my stories. I truly appreciate all my readers. ~Kay

COMFORT CROSSING ~ THE SERIES

The Shop on Main - Book One

The Memory Box - Book Two

The Christmas Cottage - A Holiday Novella (Book 2.5)

The Letter - Book Three

The Christmas Scarf - A Holiday Novella (Book 3.5)

The Magnolia Cafe - Book Four

The Unexpected Wedding - Book Five

The Wedding in the Grove (crossover short story between series - Josephine and Paul from The Letter.)

LIGHTHOUSE POINT ~ THE SERIES

Wish Upon a Shell - Book One

Wedding on the Beach - Book Two

Love at the Lighthouse - Book Three

Cottage near the Point - Book Four

Return to the Island - Book Five

Bungalow by the Bay - Book Six

Christmas Comes to Lighthouse Point - Book Seven

CHARMING INN ~ Return to Lighthouse Point

One Simple Wish - Book One

Two of a Kind - Book Two

Three Little Things - Book Three

Four Short Weeks - Book Four

Five Years or So - Book Five

Six Hours Away - Book Six

Charming Christmas - Book Seven

SWEET RIVER ~ THE SERIES

A Dream to Believe in - Book One

A Memory to Cherish - Book Two

A Song to Remember - Book Three

A Time to Forgive - Book Four

A Summer of Secrets - Book Five

A Moment in the Moonlight - Book Six

MOONBEAM BAY ~ THE SERIES

The Parker Women - Book One

The Parker Cafe - Book Two

A Heather Parker Original - Book Three

The Parker Family Secret - Book Four

Grace Parker's Peach Pie - Book Five

The Perks of Being a Parker - Book Six

BLUE HERON COTTAGES ~ THE SERIES

Memories of the Beach - Book One

Walks along the Shore - Book Two

Bookshop near the Coast - Book Three

Restaurant on the Wharf - Book Four

Lilacs by the Sea - Book Five

Flower Shop on Magnolia - Book Six

Christmas by the Bay - Book Seven

Sea Glass from the Past - Book Eight

MAGNOLIA KEY ~ THE SERIES

Saltwater Sunrise - Book One

Encore Echoes - Book Two

Coastal Candlelight - Book Three

Tidal Treasures - Book Four

Bayside Beginnings - Book Five

Seaside Sunshine - Book Six

Boardwalk Breezes - Book Seven

STARLIGHT SHORE ~ THE SERIES

Lighthouse Cottages - Book One

Harbor Festival - Book Two

CHRISTMAS SEASHELLS AND SNOWFLAKES

Seaside Christmas Wishes

Sweet River Holiday Homecoming

WIND CHIME BEACH ~ A stand-alone novel

INDIGO BAY ~

Sweet Days by the Bay - Kay's complete collection of stories in the Indigo Bay series

ABOUT THE AUTHOR

Kay Correll is a USA Today bestselling author of sweet, heartwarming stories that are a cross between women's fiction and contemporary romance. She is known for her charming small towns, quirky townsfolk, and the enduring strong friendships between the women in her books.

Kay splits her time between the southwest coast of Florida and the Midwest of the U.S. and can often be found out and about with her camera, taking a myriad of photographs, often incorporating them into her book covers. When not lost in her writing or photography, she can be found spending time with her ever-supportive husband, knitting, or playing with her puppies - a cavalier who is too cute for his own good and a naughty but adorable Australian shepherd. Their five boys are all grown now and while she misses the rowdy boy-noise chaos, she is thoroughly enjoying her empty nest years.

Learn more about Kay and her books at
kaycorrell.com

While you're there, sign up for her newsletter to
hear about new releases, sales, and giveaways.

WHERE TO FIND ME:
My shop: shop.kaycorrell.com
My author website: kaycorrell.com
authorcontact@kaycorrell.com

Join my Facebook Reader Group. We have lots of
fun and you'll hear about sales and new releases
first!
www.facebook.com/groups/KayCorrell/

I love to hear from my readers. Feel free to contact
me at authorcontact@kaycorrell.com

facebook.com/KayCorrellAuthor
instagram.com/kaycorrell
pinterest.com/kaycorrellauthor
amazon.com/author/kaycorrell
bookbub.com/authors/kay-correll

9 781966 284178